SEANCES & SECOND LINE PARADES

TWISTED SISTERS' MIDLIFE MAELSTROM BOOK 3

BRENDA TRIM

"Sometimes life gives you a second chance, or even two! Not always, but sometimes. It's what you do with those second chances that counts." - Dave Wilson.

CHAPTER 1

DANIELLE

"*I*'d feel better if I went in with you guys. There could be ghosts in there." Maliko told Dea as he pulled up to the curb outside of the One Stop Shop at City Hall.

"Somehow, I'll manage. My sisters have magic like me, babe. They can help if things go sideways," Dea replied before she leaned over and gave him a kiss.

I loved seeing Deandra happy. She'd come a long way from her troubled teen years. Dea was the last of us to get married a few years ago. She had her first son at seventeen followed by another two a few years after that.

We had watched her struggle for years and couldn't be prouder of the hard work she put in to turn her life around. She met Maliko in the process and the two of them were one of the cutest couples I knew.

Maliko was an islander with a laid-back attitude and a deep soul. He was on the shorter side for a guy, but he was fit, which made up for it. Add to that his dark complexion, black hair and dark eyes and he was a good-looking guy and he loved our sister deeply. He'd become even more over-protective than usual since our magic was unlocked.

Lia patted Maliko on the shoulder. "We're going into a government establishment for a permit not paying Marie Leveau a visit."

I hid my smirk as we got out of the car. When Maliko discovered we needed to go to the permit office for our latest client and that Dea was coming with us because she was friends with one of the clerks, he'd insisted on driving us.

Maliko waved. "I'll be back to pick you guys up shortly. You want coconut water, babe?"

Dea smiled at her husband. "Unless you find a margarita where you stop, that'll work."

"I'll grab a tall boy and an energy drink for you guys, as well," Maliko called out before he pulled away from the curb.

Dea laughed and shook her head. "That man, I swear. He's been impossible at times."

Lia adjusted my bag on her shoulder and pulled the folder out. "He's worried about you. You're part of a world that he isn't, and when you struggle, there is nothing he can do to help. He's doing what he can."

Dea's powers had been emerging increasingly and making it difficult for her to walk the line between the mundie world and the magical one. It was something we'd been working on as much as her busy life allowed. And, Maliko was having just as hard of a time adjusting.

"He's not hurting anyone by driving you around. He still gives you the space you need," I pointed out. She was like the rest of us: fiercely independent yet co-dependent.

We wanted to be free to do what we wanted while having each other do it with us. It likely made no sense to most, but that's what made us the Six Twisted Sisters. All that mattered were that my sisters' husbands had come to understand and appreciate what we had with each other.

Dea shrugged. "He asks me every few hours if there are ghosts in the house, and he vacillates between anxious, excited, and terrified. It's hard to know he's afraid of the changes."

I placed a hand on Dea's shoulder. "You've always been tuned into everyone's emotions. It's got to be difficult actually knowing how people feel now."

We'd called Kaitlyn when Deandra's symptoms started getting worse. She was the one that confirmed Dea was an empath as well as having some necromancer skills with ghosts and spirits.

We were truly mutts of the magical world. So far, we'd shown signs of nearly every magical species out there save for vampires. It had been exciting to see how each of us was developing until Deandra started experiencing all the horrendous emotions of her patients. The focus during magical practice last time had shifted to how to control the input so she could get a handle on things before it drove her crazy.

She snorted. "You have no idea. It's gut wrenching to feel the anger and resentment of those newly diagnosed as terminal. Enough of that. We need to go see Shannon and get our permit for this second line parade. Were you guys able to find a band?"

I happily made the shift. The only second line parade we'd done was the one for Lia's late husband. We hadn't done one for a customer and I was excited to do one without the sadness permeating the process.

Although, I had to admit that it would have been nice if we were planning the parade for a wedding, as is typically the case nowadays. But it was still fun to help our client plan the perfect event to honor her mother.

"Phi received confirmation yesterday. It's not the same one we used for Leo. She told me the name. It's here somewhere." Lia opened the folder and flipped through the pages that included the route that we'd planned through the Quarter along with our parade escorts and the name of the brass band we'd arranged.

Dea pulled the door open as we reached the building. "Don't worry about it. You have the application, correct? Because Shannon can't help without that."

I moved around her and entered the office without touching anything. I'd taken to wearing gloves around the house to avoid triggering my magic, but out in public it was harder to explain why I had leather gloves on. Especially in the middle of the hot summer months.

Lia lifted a piece of paper in the air triumphantly but her response was cut off when Dea gasped and froze in place. I moved closer to her and touched her arm. "Are you okay, Dea?"

"There are ghosts everywhere. Can't you see them?" Dea's face had blanched of color.

I scanned the room. The office looked like any government agency with a counter where clerks assisted people and chairs situated in the space on the other side. The information desk was set off to the side along with forms of all kinds. The place was filled with mundies and smelled like despair and boredom, if those emotions had a scent.

I didn't see one ghost which was unusual for New Orleans. We had a rich history and plenty of spirits that have stuck around for centuries. What was crazy was that before stepping foot on Willowberry, I had never seen one before. Our mom and Dea were the only ones that had previously seen one.

When Phoebe unlocked our magic, we gained more than just powers. However, paranormals could only see certain types of spirits lingering on this side. No one had been able to explain to us why Dea could see what others couldn't. That was typically the power of a necromancer. Her having it was part of that mixed breed heritage in our family.

"I don't see a thing," I told her.

Dea's eyes unfocused as she concentrated on creating an aura around herself that would repel the ghosts. Temperance, the necromancer that Phoebe had freed from Marie Leveau's control, was helping Dea learn skills to deal with this aspect of her magic.

I couldn't see what she was doing but I felt the warmth and tingle of her power as it took effect. A second later Dea put a smile on her face and crossed the lobby to the line of people waiting to be helped.

A middle-aged Hispanic woman stood up from a desk behind the counter and waved at us. Shannon's smile was bright as she gestured to the left where there was a door marked employees only.

We followed Dea and met the woman the second she flung the panel open. "Dea! How are you doing? You've missed the past two girls' night out."

Dea laughed, but it wasn't her usual infectious amusement that made you want to join her. "I've had to work doubles with the nursing shortage. And then there is the plantation. If I'm not at the hospital, I'm at Willowberry."

Shannon sucked in a breath. "That's right. How's that going? I really need to get out there and see the place." She gestured for us to follow her to her desk. I kept my arms folded over my chest with my hands tucked under my armpits.

"It's going better than we expected," I admitted. I left out the fact that most of our customers were magical creatures that would make her crap her pants.

Lia nodded as she took a seat in one of the chairs

Shannon grabbed for us. "We've hired a woman to start running tours during the day and Dre and Steve moved into one of the buildings."

Dea jerked her arm toward her chest making Shannon frown at her. Crap, the spirits must be bothering her. I reached for her then let my hand drop. Being psychometric wasn't all it's cracked up to be. I looked forward to the time I could let my guard down at home. Kaitlyn had assured me that I would eventually become immune to my environment.

I smiled, hoping it didn't look too strained. "Of course, not all of our events are being held at the plantation which is why we are here. Our client, Ava wants a second line for her mom Olivia; who recently passed but it's less than two weeks away."

Shannon winced as she turned off her screen saver. "That could be a problem. The city is careful about the timing of these and the routes taken."

"You know we can't bring you an easy request," Dea laughed.

Shannon rolled her eyes then accepted the papers from Lia. "Let's see what we can do. It's possible you will need to move the event. I know it isn't ideal but if your client is set on having a second line, it might be necessary."

I moved my seat closer to Dea as she batted at something to the side of her chair. Shannon was busy typing on her computer. I nudged Lia and jerked my head in Dea's direction then back at Shannon.

Lia's eyes flared before she nodded. She leaned forward and grabbed a frame from the desk, keeping her body angled so she hid Dea from view. "Is this Frankie now? Man, he's gotten so big. I remember when he was just a little guy running around the park."

Shannon stopped typing to smile. "Can you believe he's thirteen now? He actually made me breakfast Sunday morning and brought it to me on a tray. The pancakes were good, too."

"You're doing something right, then," Lia replied. "My kids are all too busy to stop and think about making mom a bowl of cereal let alone pancakes. Although, Eli does make a mean grilled cheese sandwich."

I made an appreciative noise thinking about the sandwich Lia's son had made me a few weeks ago right before we moved into the plantation. "They are delicious. He adds cheese to the outside too and cooks it until it's crunchy so you have that layer plus the gooey center. Oh, and then there's the hint of truffle salt."

Shannon and Lia talked cheese while Shannon went back to work. I turned and checked on Dea. She was sitting there with her hands clenched into fists. Sweat dotted her brow and her mouth was pinched.

Whatever was happening, it was triggering Dea's magic and draining her. None of us were experienced enough to shut it down at home during magical practice. Forget about the stress of being in a public place where one of your close friends was helping you. The situation was the perfect storm.

Shannon's voice made my head turn in her direction. "You're in luck. Your route and day are free. I am sliding you into the slot and granting your permit now."

"Thank God," Dea replied. "Losing your mom is tough enough."

Shannon gave Dea the smile people got when you lost a loved one. It displayed their unease more than sympathy for what you were going through. It screamed I have no idea what to say to you right now.

Cold air suddenly surrounded me making me shiver. It would have been perfect if I was having one of the never-ending hot flashes. Lia did the same thing and glanced around as surreptitiously as possible.

7

"There goes the air conditioner again. I swear they need another HVAC guy. The temperature shouldn't fluctuate this much," Shannon observed as she typed several more things then pressed a button.

The whir of the printer behind her started up a second later before it spit out several pages. Shannon picked them up and handed them over. I kept my hands tucked in my lap while Lia accepted them and tucked them into the folder.

Dea stood up when Shannon did and hugged her. "Thanks, girl. We owe you one."

Shannon chuckled. "You can repay me by joining us for taco Tuesday next week. Oh, and tell your clients they can't cut it so close next time."

"I'll be there," Dea promised her friend as she walked us to the door. I shivered as the cold intensified to the point that it burned while also chilling me to the bone.

Deandra grabbed my arm and tugged me to the bathroom to the right of the entrance. Lia moved ahead of us and pushed the door open. I bent to check under the stall doors to see if anyone was in there.

I shook my head to let them know there was still someone in one of the stalls. I leaned against the wall next to the sink where Dea washed her hands. Lia hovered nearby as she stuffed the folder back inside her bag.

"Hold this for me, sestra," Lia said to Dea.

Dea finished drying her hands then took the strap while Dahlia entered a stall. While Lia relieved herself the other woman finished up, washed her hands and left. Dea was scowling at thin air by the time Lia came out.

Dea paced back and forth. "What will it take for you to leave me alone? I'm not some ghost whisperer here to do your bidding. I wish you'd just freaking leave me alone."

Dahlia met my gaze in the mirror as she washed her hands. I lifted one shoulder but remained silent. Dea stopped, shook her head and thrust her hands on her hips. "I'm not going to act as your spokesperson with your sister. I'm sorry you're dead, but there is nothing I can do for you."

I was surprised to hear our happy sister sound irritated and upset. Dea laughed more often than not and rarely got testy with people. This ghost thing really was pushing her to the edge of her sanity.

The color drained from Dea's face and her hand flew to her mouth. "How are you bound together? I don't understand."

I straightened off the wall. "What is it?"

Dea waved her arm through the air. "Giselle here says that she needs help contacting her twin sister, Georgette, because the two of them are bound together."

Lia's forehead furrowed. "How will contacting her help? It'll only cause any grief she's lived with to resurface. That will make it harder to learn to cope without her sister."

Dea wrapped her arms around her torso. "She says her sister will lose her mind to madness unless I help them."

This had become our life lately. We'd encounter any number of supernatural events while out trying to do normal mundane things, like obtain a permit for a parade. Just like the vision Dahlia had been hit with a couple weeks ago about a dead woman being dumped on Canal Street, this request from a ghost came out of the blue.

I pinched the bridge of my nose. "I suppose this isn't something we can ignore. So, how do we help her? Does she know where to find her sister?"

The door opened making all three of us jump out of our skin. The woman who had come in stopped and took a step back. "Is, uh, everything alright in here?"

I smiled at her and gestured to Dea who was still pale and shaken. "We're great. My sister here was just telling us the

9

ghost story about what this place was used for and it shook us."

The woman's eyes went wide and she looked around. "You must be some story teller. What was it used for? I haven't heard anything about this building."

Deandra rubbed her hands theatrically. "It wasn't the office, but the location. Rumor has it this was the site of a bloody battle between the English and the French. I don't know how true it is, but my friend said hundreds of soldiers died here and still haunt the location. But she must be wrong. You don't see any ghosts, do you?"

My heart was racing and my mind pondered the accuracy of Dea's story. Battles had been fought all over our fair city at one point or another, so the chances were high that she was telling the truth.

I had never seen the ghost of a soldier. From her description, it seemed like perhaps she had. It made me wonder if their wounds were visible after they died and came back a ghost.

The woman shook her head. "Not one. Some of the stories in this city are outrageous. Don't believe half of what you hear. It's great for tourism but that's about it."

Lia and I laughed as the lady went into one of the stalls. Lia, who was standing next to the sink, turned on the faucet and proceeded to wash her hands. She took her time scrubbing them until after the woman left.

Lia shifted her gaze to Dea with pursed lips. "Was your story true? And how can we find this sister fast? We need to get the hell out of here before someone else comes in."

Dea blew out a breath. "It's difficult to communicate with ghosts. Giselle hasn't managed to tell me more than their first names."

My shoulders sagged and I moved to leave. "We will have

to deal with this later. Tell her we will come back." The evil side of me silently added, or not.

"She's not happy about that idea," Dea replied.

I clenched my jaw shut. "Explain to her this isn't the place to get into this with her. If she persists, she could get us committed."

"She heard you and said she will come with us." Dea moved around me to open the door. The panel slammed into the wall as she yanked it open.

Lia gasped and glanced around. "She can't do that."

We were close to the exit, so it didn't take us long before we were outside on the sidewalk. Dea searched for Maliko. "I don't think she cares about what she can and can't do, Lia. Her spirit is following me. Shit, we need to do something. You can't come home with me, Giselle. Maliko will rethink how much he loves me if I start bringing ghosts home like lost dogs."

My heart squeezed hearing the frantic worry in my sister's voice. "We can bring her back to Willowberry. There are plenty of places outside the main house where she can haunt."

Deandra waved at Maliko who was parked a few feet in front of us at the curb. "I owe you both big time. You're saving me a huge headache."

I pulled my gloves out and slipped them on so I didn't catch a glimpse of something in Maliko's car. The last thing I needed was to add to the headache blooming behind my eyes. "Tell her to follow us to the plantation."

I thanked Maliko for the tall boy he'd picked up for me and considered taking a swig of Dea's margarita. This day had already been eventful and it was still early.

CHAPTER 2

DAHLIA

"*I* can't wait to get shopping! Are you ready, sestras?" Kota called out enthusiastically.

She wasn't the hardest working in our motley crew, but she was always up for an adventure, especially when it involved shopping. Zoe one of my French bulldogs jumped up when she heard her voice and raced out of the room.

I bent and scratched Oscar's head as he watched his sister. I imagined him debating if it was worth the effort. He would have been tearing through the house if it had been a stranger. "Yep, we're in the kitchen trying to convince Cami and Dre to go with us."

"What do you mean? Of course, they're going." Dakota entered in her stretchy pants and loose t-shirt.

Dre shook her head, sending her blonde locks flying. "I'm going to stick around and help Steve with the addition to our house. The kids can't bring the grand babies over until we have a space where they can take naps." Dre and Steve had married when they were eighteen years old and had their first child a year later, so she already had grandkids.

Camilla was wringing her hands together as she sat at the kitchen table with us. She wasn't related to us by blood but we'd adopted her into the family, after Phoebe raised her as a ghoul in the process of breaking the curse on our plantation. It was during that process that she'd also unlocked the dormant magic in our DNA.

"I can't go shopping for magical supplies. It wouldn't be proper." Cami was born several hundred years ago to a slave and the wife of the man who had built this plantation. Her short life had been traumatic as she was forced to be a slave for her own mother and then was killed young. Her mother haunted Willowberry to this day wanting to form a real relationship with Cami.

Dani sighed and patted Cami's shoulder. "You know times are different now. It's perfectly acceptable for you to go shopping with us."

Cami chewed on her lip so hard I thought she would draw blood. Dre stood up and gestured to Cami. "You don't have to go. You can help Steve and I. The boys aren't here today, so we could use the help."

Dre was the mother of our group and looked out for each of us. It made me smile to see that Cami was no different. Cami bolted from her chair. "I'd love to learn how to use more of the power tools. It makes jobs so much easier now."

I shrugged my shoulder. "Suit yourselves. Do you have any requests?"

Dre took her cup to the sink and rinsed it out. "Nothing aside from what Kaitlyn told us to get for our magical kitchen." That's what Dakota had decided to call the space we would use to store our magical accoutrement and create potions when we started that work.

Dani, Kota, and I said goodbye to Cami and Dre then

headed to the French Quarter. We were heading to Solid Solutions, the store owned by Hollie Johnson. She was a witch in our coven, but we didn't really know her all that well.

My sisters piled into my SUV and I drove us to the lower section of the Quarter. Solid Solutions was located outside the busiest section. I often wondered why the supernaturals set up so many businesses in an area thousands of mundies visited on a daily basis.

Admittedly, the risk of discovery was lower in our fair city. We were known for being a paranormal hotspot. Marie Leveau was the first to bring that reputation to the area. Others, like Anne Rice only added more to the local lore.

I parked at the lot on Ursulines, near Chartres. The buildings and pavement trapped the heat and it was hot as hell. The breeze, from the river a few blocks over, was the only reprieve we got.

Solid Solutions was in a narrow, brightly colored row house. I loved everything about New Orleans, particularly the French Quarter. A smile spread over my face as I got out and looked at the pink and green structure. There was no neon sign in the window. Nor was there a wooden one hanging outside. I double checked to make sure we were in the right place.

Dani considered her gloves then shrugged. "I'm leaving them on in here."

Kota climbed the stairs to the door. I noted there was a small sign with the name of the place, with a pentagram and the letter o, in the words. "That's smart. This place has seen its fair share of visitors. God knows what you'd see in here."

I was jealous that Dani had a way to block her power. My weird scent ability tended to hit me from out of nowhere, without warning. I simply had to roll with it. Being caught in a vision around strangers was my least favorite thing in the world. It left me and my sisters vulnerable.

A chime tinkled as we walked through the door and into the cool interior of the shop. I was immediately over-whelmed by the sheer amount of stuff surrounding us. Some shelves were full of jars with herbs in them. Others had black cauldrons, candles, and crystals on them. There was a glass display case with athames and tarot cards. There were even a few crystal balls.

A young woman that was around our height, with light brown hair pulled into a ponytail, pushed her way through a beaded curtain from the back. I didn't recognize Hollie with her hair pulled back. She also didn't have the thick black eye makeup on today. "Welcome to Solid Solutions. How can I help you?"

Kota put the silk cloth she was holding back on the shelf. "I hope so. We're here to buy magical supplies."

Hollie scrutinized us. I wondered what she was thinking. She was half our age, in leggings and a crop top, while we were wearing the same type of bottoms but had shirts big enough to be circus tents. "You're the Twisted Sisters, aren't you? Kaitlyn said I should be expecting you."

Dani inclined her head. "That's us. I'm glad Kaitlyn called you. It's always awkward explaining who we are to new people, and why they've never met us before."

Hollie laughed as she joined us in the middle of the place. "I can only imagine. The magical world is very excited about you six. We've never had anywhere that we can hold our events. Let alone a place that has been warded by the Pleiades. I know of a dozen that want to use Willowberry because it's a safe place to have a party. I'm Hollie, by the way."

I winced at her words. Yes, Willowberry had strong

protections surrounding the property, but we could still be attacked as was evidenced by the zombies and sirens that had infiltrated the plantation a few weeks ago. The loophole for the walking dead was their lack of life, and the latter because they meant us no harm.

"I'm Dahlia, and this is Danielle and Dakota. You must not have heard about Nedasea's party then. We have impenetrable wards around the property but had to leave the section along the parking lot and entrance loose. We're looking for ways to shore those up but haven't found anything yet. We're still learning."

Hollie waved her hand dismissively. "Kaitlyn said that will be fixed shortly. No one will hold that against you."

"They haven't yet. Requests from the magical world continue to pick up steam," Dani replied. "We have this list of what we need. And we will be back another time to get what we'll need when we hold one of the festivals for the coven."

Hollie took the list from Dani. "I'd be honored to help you with the festival preparations. And this list is exactly what I was expecting you to need. I've actually already put your supplies together." Her cheeks pinkened as she admitted that to us.

Dakota glanced around with a pout on her face. "Oh, thanks. That makes this trip faster."

Hollie's brow furrowed. "But what I didn't select were items you want to practice making charms with. I have several styles to choose from and didn't want to be presumptuous. I also didn't know if you had a desire for crystals you might want to place around your house. Training starts with the basics."

Kota brightened when she heard that. "Can you show us the charms?"

Hollie disappeared behind the beads again and I shot

wide eyes to my sisters. "This is insane. I feel like a celebrity or something."

Dani snorted. "Celebrities aren't asked to do shit for people. I'm just waiting to hear what kind of party she wants to throw."

Kota smelled a red candle then put it back on the shelf. "That is true. But it's what we do. Oh, look at this. We need it for our magical kitchen."

Dakota was looking at a white ceramic hand that had symbols in various places across the palm and fingers. I had no idea what it all meant or what it might be used for, but she was the decorator in our group.

I shrugged my shoulders. "Sounds good to me. Maybe that silk tablecloth, too."

Dani picked a different silk and held it up. "I like this one better. The black, gold and teal will look good in the space. We can even add a teal accent wall."

Dani loved doing projects and was nearly as good at decorating as Kota. Dakota outshone Dani in the ability to have fifty items on and around a sofa table and still make it look good.

Hollie returned before the two of them could get distracted with decorating the kitchen. "Here we are." The shopkeeper set four wood trays on the glass counter top. Each one had a couple dozen sections with different charms in each one.

Kota picked up a small silver bee. "This is the one. We all have to have one. We can get others but we need a sestra one."

Hollie chuckled. "You call each other sestra, too? My sister and I do, as well. I've never considered creating a sisters' charm. I love the idea. You could have it protect the bond you share or prohibit anyone from sowing discord."

We readily agreed and each selected several other charms, including a couple for Cami. After Kota added a few items for décor, I pulled out my wallet to pay so we could leave. I held my breath as we waited to hear our total.

My mouth dropped open when Hollie told me it was all under five hundred dollars. "Are you sure you didn't miss anything? That seems low for what we got." I'd figured it would cost at least two to three hundred for each of us.

"I'm sure. Coven members get a discount. You guys are my bread and butter and I like to show my appreciation for you shopping here," Hollie replied. "Now, let me help you out with these boxes."

I was about to tell her we could get it when she went through the beads then shoved six banker boxes through to the main room. On second thought, she could help. "Thanks a million."

Hollie picked one up as I grabbed one and handed it to Dani, then another and handed it to Kota. When each of us had one in our hands, we took them to the car. I ran back with Dani to get the last two boxes. After thanking Hollie again, Dani and I went back to the car.

I had just stepped foot on the sidewalk when something seized me, making it impossible to move. "Dani!"

As my sister turned around, a far too familiar face blocked my view of her and shoved me against the building making me drop the box of supplies. The sound of glass breaking was loud in the afternoon. My heart dropped to my feet when I looked into Marie Leveau's grey eyes.

The hair on my arms prickled, and it felt like ants were crawling all over me. The look on her face made my stomach twist into knots. Dani and Kota came running up to us. Marie flicked her arm in their direction. Her numerous bracelets jangled and my sisters stopped a foot away. Were they frozen, too?

"What do you want? You're taking a big risk attacking me like this on the street where mundies can see." My insides were shaking like a 5.0 earthquake along a fault line. I was no match for this powerful woman, yet I couldn't show her my fear.

Marie glared daggers at me. "I want to know why you and your sisters are spreading rumors that I attacked the six of you."

I took a second to think about a bubble of protection around my body and silently chanted the spell hoping I could cast it. "None of us have spread rumors. Zombies attacked Willowberry. That didn't happen by accident."

Marie bared her teeth and wrapped her hand around my throat. "How dare you talk to me like that. I haven't been near your plantation since that night I was invited. And I have not ordered your attack."

I couldn't tell if the pressure around my throat was getting tighter or if I was simply having a hard time breathing due to fright. "I didn't realize your mambos acted without your permission. Or perhaps you have a new best friend in town and she hasn't received the memo about not attacking others."

Marie's eyes narrowed and I felt the heat from her power crackling against my skin. "You're not a funny woman, Dahlia. I am the Queen of Voodoo. Nothing happens in my territory without me knowing."

I smirked at her. "Then you are aware of the attack against us. Tell me, if it wasn't you then who was it?"

Marie clenched her jaw so tight I heard something crack. "You will do well to watch your words. I am a queen, not a goddess. I cannot control my mambos. It's entirely possible one was practicing and her zombies got out of her control."

I rolled my eyes then gasped when the pressure definitely increased. Marie's magic made my entire body itch and burn like I'd contracted a case of crabs that covered my entire body.

"That's the biggest load of bullshit I've ever heard. You control half of this city's supernaturals and you have the other half terrified of what you will do to them. Speaking of which, did it hurt to lose the necromancers?" I hoped my words reminded the bitch that she wasn't all that powerful anymore.

My sisters were shaking their heads back and forth and mouthing for me to shut my trap before I got us killed. I understood their fear. I was one second from crapping my pants. However, I'd dealt with bullies in my career as a social worker. You couldn't back down and let them see they hurt you. It only fueled their desire to inflict more pain. Regardless of the situation, people paused when faced with confidence and insolence. After all, if you couldn't fight back why would you say anything?

I was taking a risk and pissing off a very powerful woman. The thing was, she already hated us because we were instrumental in thwarting her plans to bring one of the loa through and stick it in Selene or Camilla's body. She hated us for preventing her god from getting a foothold on Earth. What I was saying now didn't change that.

My oxygen was cut off as Marie's hand tightened enough that the tips of her nails dug into my skin. Her death magic seemed to suck the life out of me. "You six might have magic now, but you're weak. Barely more than mundies. You might have had power in the mundane world, but you don't in the magical one. You had better watch yourselves. You have no idea who you are messing with. You will have no doubt if I am behind an attack on you."

Kota glared daggers at Marie. "Sounds like you need to clean house. For someone who's supposed to have all this power, your own people are acting without permission. You should look within because like Lia said, all we have done is share that we were attacked by zombies which is a fact."

My anger rose and I acted on instinct. Light burst from my hands, burning through the magical binds on my wrists. I heard a gasp above us along with the words 'angelic light.' Part of my mind made note of it while the rest soaked up the energy from the illumination. It was filled with life and love, everything anathema to Marie Leveau's power.

Marie yanked her hand back with a hiss, releasing me. I stalked toward her at the same time Kota and Dani called their witch fire to their hands and came at her from behind. "This isn't over, witches."

I dropped the light and sagged against the building. Hollie came running outside. "How did you call angel light? I've only read about it in books."

Dani, Kota, and I shared a confused look. I shrugged my shoulders. "We seem to have a little of every supernatural in us, so who knows where it came from. I'm just glad it was enough to make her leave."

Hollie rubbed her arms. "You six have made a powerful enemy."

Dani blanched. "We did that when we stopped her from stealing Selene or Camilla's body for her loa. You have to stand up to bullies or they will run your life whether you like it or not."

Hollie smiled at that. "Seeing you stand up to her was fantastic! I've never seen anyone make her back down. And you're right, Dani. This city has bowed to her long enough. You guys are my new idols."

I smiled, unsure what to say to that as I picked up the box. Something was definitely broken inside. We said our good-byes and headed to the car. I wondered how soon word would get around and how this incident would be recounted. I wasn't sure if I hoped people said we'd kicked Marie's ass or not. Marie might have been our enemy before this, but this incident didn't help matters any. Most of the city was terrified of the Voodoo Queen for good reason. I just hoped she was a little afraid of us, as well.

CHAPTER 3

DANIELLE

"*I*'m one second from banishing you, Giselle. You've got to lay off and stop making me crazy," Dea barked at the ghost as Lia parked the car in the lot of a strip mall in Metarie.

The dark circles under Deandra's eyes and frantic expression made her look like she'd been on a bender the night before. Almost like she was doing the walk of shame without having washed up? Or was she more like a nurse that had pulled a double and hadn't slept in over twenty-four hours?

After our run in with Marie Leveau yesterday, the rest of the sisters had come over to debrief. Dre regretted not coming with us, saying she should have been there to help with the Voodoo Queen. No one could have foreseen the incident. I was just grateful Kota and I were there with Lia.

Ever since Lia was attacked a few weeks ago and nearly killed, we'd promised each other we would be there for one another. Little did we know our lives were going to be full of magical intrigue and danger.

It could be a lot worse. It could be boring.

I reached between the seats and placed my hand on her shoulder before she got out of the car. "While we can't make this any easier for you, Lia and I are here for you to pretend you're talking to us. That will help if you have to say anything to Giselle while we are inside."

Dea laughed as she opened the passenger door of Lia's car. "That's everything. It's just hard to hear Giselle's constant nagging and feel her fear at the same time. It's all-consuming and difficult to cope with. It goes well beyond normal emotions. There's this air of desperation that makes me restless."

Lia's face scrunched up. "Is it like she's being driven to act? Could there be foreign influence at work here?"

Dea touched the side of her nose. "I think you hit the nail on the head there, but I can't get Giselle to stop freaking out long enough to give me information, let alone allow me to think straight."

"Freaking Ma...death magic. I think we all know who might be behind this," I replied as we walked toward the salon where Giselle told Dea her sister worked. "One of these days we're going to drop kick her out of our town."

Lia chuckled and nudged my shoulder. "We have powerful friends and just might be able to make that happen. For now, let's deal with what is in front of us."

Dea pulled the glass door open and held it while I walked into the salon. The smell of bleach, color, and shampoo greeted me like a long, lost friend. I'd gone to beauty school right out of high school and became a cosmetologist only to discover the career wasn't for me.

A beautiful black woman looked up from the desk just inside the door. "Welcome to Blade. Can I help you?"

Dea stepped around me. "We're just looking for Georgette. We were hoping to talk with her."

The young woman narrowed her eyes at us. "Who are you?"

Dea smiled and kept her gaze trained on the woman. I felt the heat of her power a second later and I wondered if she was using it on the receptionist or the ghost. "We're longtime friends of the twins and wanted to check in and see how she was doing."

The receptionist's expression smoothed out as she returned the smile. "I'd love to help you but she quit a few weeks ago and didn't leave any forwarding information. Although I'm sure since you are family friends you will have other places to look."

Dea's smile crumpled as she thanked the young woman, then we left the salon. No one said anything as we got in the car. I pulled my gloves on and buckled my seat belt while my mind raced with ways to help Dea. The last thing I wanted was to fail another sister like I had Lia, when she felt she had to go looking for a killer alone and was attacked.

Deandra turned in the passenger seat and glared at the seat next to me. "You need to stop this frantic search for your sister and think about where she might be located. We can't find her without more information."

My gaze bounced between the empty seat and Deandra, despite not being able to see Giselle. Whatever the ghost was saying, it wasn't what Dea wanted to hear. I missed Dea's infectious laughter. Having magic wasn't worth it if it was going to cost us our fun-loving sister.

Deandra's attitude rarely soured. I could recall several times my other sisters had been angry, but not with Dea. She always wore a smile and saw the bright side of things.

Lia tapped her fingers on the steering wheel as she drove down the highway. "I take it Giselle isn't replying. We need to search the books for ways to calm spirits. Kota can make a batch of margaritas if you want. Or perhaps you could take a nap. You need to rest."

Dea let her head fall against the headrest. "This isn't like me. I never snap at anyone, but here I am yelling at a woman who died and is desperate to help her sister. Part of it is my frustration about not being able to get her to talk coherently."

"Let's start with you giving yourself a break. You shouldn't expect to have mastered a skill when you've never been taught the first thing about it. That's like expecting to know how to perform a tracheotomy on a patient just because you're familiar with aspects of the procedure," I countered.

Lia pulled into the parking lot and gripped Dea's hand. "Dani's right. Let's get in there and see if anyone found information that might help."

Dea wrapped me in a hug as we got out of the car. I returned her embrace before we joined the others under the covered space between the main house and the original kitchen for the plantation. We'd renovated that space for use by caterers and cooked our meals in the kitchen that had been more recently added to the main house.

Kota, Phi, and Dre were sitting at one of the tables that had been made by our grandfather. Kota lifted a glass pitcher while Phi lifted a second one. Dakota tilted the container from side to side making the green liquid slosh around. "Pick your poison, sestras. From the look on your faces, it seems the margs are in order."

Dea fell into a chair with a heavy sigh. "I hate to say it, but I'd be better off drinking one of Lia's energy drinks. I'm asleep on my feet here."

"I'll grab you one," Dahlia offered then raced into the house while Dea told the others what had happened.

Phi lifted one of the books that Kaitlyn had given us from the table. "I've looked through this and noted several pages that talk about how spirits can be disoriented right after death. Do we know when Giselle passed away? Perhaps that's causing her frantic state."

Dea shrugged her shoulders. "She says she knows she's dead but has no idea when it happened."

Dakota waved her phone. "What's her last name? I can do a quick search."

Dea's attention shifted to the left and her forehead furrowed. "She says something feels wrong. It's making her flicker in and out. Her last name is Coleman. Or maybe it's Solomon. I can't say for sure. She's hard to understand." Dea's brows furrowed like it did when she was listening to the ghost. "How do you know something is wrong? Why do you need to reach Georgette so urgently?"

Lia returned with the energy drink and placed it in front of Dea then handed me my tumbler filled with ice and a tall boy. "Have we learned anything?"

"Their last name and that's about it," I replied. The sound of the can cracking when I lifted the tab brought a smile to my face. Getting so much joy out of a drink that was bad for you was all kinds of wrong, but I took happiness where I could get it.

"Giselle says she can feel something pulling at her sister and Georgette doesn't want to go." Dea's gaze shifted to us as she explained what she'd managed to get from the ghost. "When that urge gets stronger is when Giselle seems to start freaking out because she can't find her sister. She tries to travel to where she thinks Georgette will be, but she isn't able to find her. She's been wandering the city since she died."

Dakota's eyes went wide as they lifted from the screen of her phone. "Their name is Coleman and Giselle died the night Marie Leveau tried to hijack Selene and Cami. Giselle was killed in an attack near the Quarter."

Lia leaned forward in the seat she'd taken next to me. "Do you think that's a coincidence?"

Dre poured herself a margarita. "Who the hell knows? We have to put that aside for now. It won't help us locate Georgette. Who or what has the power to control spirits like this?"

Cami came outside at that moment holding the leather-bound book I recalled finding in the wall of the house. "I'm sorry for listening in, but I think I might have found a piece of information in my family's grimoire."

Dahlia tugged a chair that was close to the house and patted the seat. "It's okay. Old habits are hard to break. But I will remind you that you can join us anytime. If we are doing a sisters' only activity then I will let you know. By the way, I'm proud of you for keeping with the reading on your own. This book couldn't have been easy for you. Now, what do you have?" Everyone agreed that Cami was family now, however, we wanted to keep her safe from the chaos that seemed to follow us.

Cami's cheeks pinkened as she dipped her head and came fully out of the house. Her mother, our resident specter, hovered in the open doorway. I was tempted to slam the panel. Mary Alice's spirit freaked me out. She was mostly silent as she brooded, trying to get closer to her daughter.

Cami flipped through several pages then set the book on the table so we could all see what she'd seen. The pages were made of old vellum and the writing was fancy script. Given how old the book was, I knew it was written with a quill and iron gall ink. It was impressive that Cami was able to read anything in the book given she was illiterate before coming back as a ghoul and subsequently getting her soul back.

"Death magic is most likely at work here. My ancestors

documented how necromancers and voodoo practitioners are the only ones capable of this power." Cami's gaze met Dea's across the table. "Although, they were ignorant in some ways because we know there can be hybrids with the ability too. I don't know if it will help, but these people can force the dead to do their bidding. And if this other passage is right, Giselle's sister is being controlled through her."

What the hell was she talking about? My focus shifted back to the book as she flipped to another page. This passage was in a different writing than the first, but was just as fancy and in the same fading ink.

It also indicated that twins were one soul that had been split into two bodies. There was documentation about how they shared everything from thoughts to powers, and what happened to one impacted another.

I'd heard of studies done where identical twins that had been separated at birth and raised by different families in separate countries. They tended to be nearly identical in their tastes, mannerisms and choices.

Dea ran a hand through her hair. "I think we need to call Tempe. This is way over our heads. Yes, we've gained information. But we all know the likeliest culprit is Marie Leveau and I am not talented enough to be able to get that information from Giselle, or get her to help us find her sister."

I nodded and pulled my phone out of my pocket, but Dakota had already dialed the necromancer that had surprisingly become our friend. "Hey Tempe, it's Kota. We have a situation here with a ghost that no one but Dea can see. Long story short, it involves a twin and possible manipulation by an outside force. Can you come by the plantation?"

Dakota nodded her head thanked the necromancer then hung up. "She's on her way. Who else wants an afternoon cocktail?"

I considered it but declined. I didn't care for tequila as much. I was a rum girl. "I'm grabbing some butter toffee peanuts. Anyone want anything?"

Requests for chips and guacamole, street tacos, beans, and rice prompted Kota and Cami to head into the kitchen and cook lunch for everyone. I could cook a handful of things, and this meal wasn't among them.

Dea and I thumbed through Cami's grimoire while the others cooked. "Let's look at that page about death magic again. There might be something you can use."

Deandra nodded and moved to the chair next to me. "I saw something about the voodoo religion and how they revered the dead. It makes sense given what we know, but it's creepy as hell."

We read for twenty minutes and looked for other references to death magic but didn't come across anything helpful. We had just closed the book when my sisters came outside carrying platters of food. At the same time, Temperance parked her car. She got out and was decked from head to toe in black. It made me sweat to see her in the dark clothing, but it worked for her.

We all waved the necromancer over and offered her some food. Instead of making herself scarce, Cami remained in her seat eating her lunch. It was good to see the former slave stepping out of her comfort zone.

Tempe threw some chicken and avocado on a corn tortilla then gestured to the left where Dea had spoken to Giselle a bit ago. "I take it this is the ghost you called me about." The necromancer's brown hair blew into her eyes with the breeze gusting through the space.

Dea nodded then told Temperance everything that had happened since we'd met her in City Hall. "I'd like to learn how to deal with spirits like her. I finally got her calm enough to give us some information but the longer she talked the more agitated she got."

Tempe chewed her taco as she listened then wiped her mouth with a napkin. "That was delicious. Thank you. I'd already eaten lunch but I can never turn down tacos."

"Who can?" Kota laughed.

Temperance's smile was reflected in her light blue eyes as she continued. "The place to start is with meditation and a spell to secure the spirit. In this case Cami is right about the connection between twins. They do share a soul, so part of what Giselle is experiencing is influenced by what her sister is going through. In this case, I will use a spell to try and protect the spirits. It's a long shot, but by protecting Giselle, I might be able to protect Georgette and if I can do that then they can give us more information."

The rest of us ate and watched as Tempe shifted her chair away from the table. She grabbed a red candle from her bag and some herbs. Her magic made my skin prickle as she added the two together then lit the flame.

She hummed beneath her breath for several minutes before she chanted something in a language other than Latin. The air chilled and Dea watched with rapt attention. I wondered what was happening. It was frustrating not to be able to see everything around us.

It made me think back to before we got our magic. We'd been ignorant to the magical world and didn't see most of what occurred in it. However, it wasn't as hard then because we had no clue this even existed.

"You died violently," Tempe presumably said to the ghost. "There's a powerful energy surrounding you."

Phi's hand flew to her chest as she watched the necromancer. "Was it the skin walker?"

Tempe shook her head. "No, the skin walker can't claim a

soul like this. Whoever did it is obscuring their identity. I'm trying to push through the spell."

Kota set her margarita down and scowled. "Seems like she who shall not be named has been a busy little beaver. I can see her having contingency plans on that night."

I inclined my head in agreement. "Her family motto seems to be use everyone and everything possible to serve the evil loa."

Tempe gasped then started trembling as her eyes turned to me. The haunted look in their blue depths chilled my blood. "You're right. This feels like a loa that has claimed Giselle's soul and is taking power from her."

Dea lifted a hand at the same time I was trying to figure out why that sounded somewhat familiar. "Wait a minute. The loa wouldn't want the spirit. They have plenty in their realm to fuel their evil needs. They were after Selene and Cami's body last time."

Temperance picked up her chair and rejoined the group. "I wasn't prepared for Marie when she tried to hijack my ritual. I should have known she had a back-up. She wouldn't want to piss off her loa by giving him hope only to fail. They would make her pay painfully for that failure. It's easier for a loa to overtake a mundie because they don't have the natural protections that a supernatural does. If you can reunite Giselle with Georgette, their spirits can reconnect and the two of them will be alright because they are two halves of a whole. If Marie's mambos knew about Georgette, they might already have her."

Dea cursed up a blue streak. "That's why Giselle is so frantic. She's sensing the danger her sister is in right now. What the hell do we do? How do we find Georgette if Marie Leveau is involved?"

No one had a response. Based on the shocked expressions, they were trying to absorb what Tempe had just told us. Anger surged through me. I didn't believe Marie for a second when she said she wasn't involved in the attack on us, and I couldn't see her mambos acting without her direction. The supernaturals in this city were all terrified of her, even those she couldn't take to task for disobeying. This had her name written all over it.

CHAPTER 4

DAHLIA

I sucked in a breath, letting out the fear that had gripped me with Tempe's words. "We have to treat this like an investigation and gather evidence and information that could lead us to Georgette. She no longer works at Blade, so we search her apartment next."

Calling Temperance was a good idea. I doubt we would have gotten the information any other way. Knowing that there was potentially a powerful god trying to take over Georgette's body took this case from a dead woman missing her sister to something far more important.

Not that we wouldn't give it as much effort if all we had discovered was a sister needing to be reconnected with her twin. The six of us understood how hard it would be to lose one another. I loved my sisters. Hell, I lived with one and couldn't imagine ever being parted again. Despite what the sexy shifter in my life might want.

Lucas and I had become more serious in the past few

weeks, but I loved living with Dani and wanted to keep it that way. Luc enhanced my life and made it better, but he wasn't the central figure around which I revolved. I'd learned, when I lost Leo, that narrowing your world to one person would end in heartache. I even went so far as to move away with Leo. After he passed away, I was left on my own with no one for support in the area. Forging new relationships with my sisters took time and was not something I was willing to jeopardize.

Temperance stood up and saluted the rest of us. "You guys are naturals at this stuff. It's no wonder you thwarted a skin walker and a clan of sirens while also throwing a killer party. I'll leave you all to it. Let's catch up later, Dea, and I can go over some more tricks with you. Your instincts are spot on. With a bit of training in meditation and spells, you'll be a real asset to your coven. In fact, they'll be the only ones in the world to welcome someone with necromancer powers."

There was no mistaking the bitterness in her tone. "Why aren't you part of the coven here? Is it because you used to be under Marie's thumb?"

Tempe tilted her head to the side and considered me. After a few seconds she lifted one shoulder. "It's been this way my entire life. My mom told me the witches are afraid of death magic, but I don't think that's the entire story. Witches are terrified of our ability to bring them back as ghouls after they pass on. They're also frightened of the few of my kind that were bad. Centuries ago, someone decided all necromancers would manipulate ghosts and bring witches back to be their slaves."

"That's as bad as the treatment of black people centuries ago. At least mundies have evolved and recognized their mistakes." Delphine crossed her arms over her chest and growled. "I'm honestly surprised witches haven't already tried to bridge the gap between the two groups. In our short time in the magical world, we've needed you several times. Statistically, that can't be an anomaly."

Temperance placed her hand on Phi's arm. "Thank you for recognizing that. Perhaps you six will be the ones to bring about change in our world."

Dre chuckled. "If anyone can do it, we can. Besides, as we've been reminded recently, we've made some powerful friends that might be able to help the cause."

"I'd love to be a part of it, as well," Tempe replied. "Anyway, I will see you guys later."

Dani picked up one of the lunch platters and headed for the kitchen. "Are we all going to the apartment?"

The rest of us each picked up some of the dishes and followed Dani inside. Dre set hers in the sink and turned to grab some storage containers for the leftovers. "I think we should all go along. I've been thinking that we might not find anything. It can't hurt to reach out to Kaitlyn and ask if we can stop by after, so she can help us scry using something of Georgette's."

I paused in washing one of the platters. "That's actually a great idea. What are the chances Georgette wasn't taken from her place, given that Giselle was killed downtown? I was worried we wouldn't find anything to help us. Now it won't be a wasted trip at all."

Dani set the container of meat in the fridge. "I see one problem with this plan. How the hell do we get into this woman's apartment? None of us has a key."

"Breaking and entering? Holy crap. I can't wear orange," Kota replied. "It's not my color."

Dea laughed in response and her infectious laugh had all of us giggling until we couldn't breathe. When we subsided, Dea opened the window. "Can you tell us how to get into your sister's house?"

Giselle had followed our conditions and remained outside ever since she came home with us two days before. I appreciated it. Mary Alice didn't seem like the kind of woman that shared her space very well.

A grin spread over Dea's mouth. Whatever Giselle said it must be good news. "The two of them lived in one half of a shotgun house in Mid-City and they have a digital lock with a code to get inside."

"And she was able to tell you the code?" Dani asked with a frown. I understood her doubt. The ghost hadn't been able to communicate much.

Dea pursed her lips. "Ever since Tempe did her thing, Giselle has been calm and clear. Necro magic for the win on this one. We would have been breaking a window to get inside if she hadn't quieted Giselle's chaos."

Dakota waved her phone in the air. "Mid-City isn't that far from the Garden District where Kaitlyn is located. I sent her a text message that we'd like to stop by later this afternoon."

I finished washing the last of the dishes, hopeful that we would be able to get some answers for Giselle soon. "Do you want to drive, Phi? Or should I?"

Delphine and I were typically the ones to drive when we all went someplace together. Phi grabbed her iPad and purse. "I'll drive this time. You took them this morning."

We said goodbye to Cami while Dre let Steve know where we were going. Dani pulled on her gloves and a few seconds later we were loaded into the car with Phi as she backed out of the lot. She turned right onto the street and headed to Giselle and Georgette's house.

On the way, Dani discussed the tasks that still needed to be done for the second line parade for Olivia. Her favorite flower was a hydrangea but finding nice ones in bloom this late in the summer in New Orleans could be a chore. Dani was the master at finding what clients wanted and by the time we made it to Mid-City she had several blue hydrangeas on order for the event.

Delphine managed to find street parking a couple of houses down from Giselle and Georgette's house which was a small miracle. We all hopped out of the car and headed for the blue shotgun house. Dea handled unlocking the entrance and we all followed her inside praying the neighbors across the street didn't come over and ask us questions. When my eyes adjusted to the darker interior, I couldn't believe what we were seeing.

"Either Georgette had one helluva party or someone paid her an unwanted visit," Kota observed. I could see her fingers twitch as she glanced around the mess before us.

I wasn't the best housekeeper on the planet. That designation belonged to Dakota. Her house was decorated to the hilt and always immaculate. I used her as a bar for my own place. It used to make me get off the chair and stop working long enough to dust the mantle off and clean the toilets. After years of feeling inadequate, I decided I was going to pay someone to help me with the heavy-duty stuff while I did my best to keep stuff neat. The kids made keeping it pristine impossible. Without the kids around, Dani and I were able to keep the plantation house in much better shape.

I continued through the living room to check the first bedroom and found it in the same condition. The second bedroom fared a little better but the kitchen was a disaster. "It's like they were looking for something. Can you ask Giselle if they were into anything illegal?"

Dea rolled her eyes but did as I requested. "Giselle assures me they lived a normal, quiet life. She's getting agitated again. I can't tell if Tempe's spell is wearing off or if she's just too close to the power of the loa."

Dani picked up a hair brush and gestured with it. "Grab

anything that looks suspicious. If it has blood on it, grab it. It might not belong to Georgette but her kidnapper."

Everyone started sifting through things. I started in the second bedroom with Deandra and was quickly over-whelmed with grief. These two women were indeed close. There were pictures of them all over the place and in each one they were laughing or smiling.

Seeing how intertwined their lives were, it made me think of Dani and I living together at Willowberry while running this business with our other sisters. I wouldn't change where I was at for anything in the world. I loved my life now. I had space when I needed it but I didn't have to be alone if I didn't want to be. And a sexy shifter that was crazy about me. Plus, a successful business.

I noticed a t-shirt that had splatters of blood on it, so I snagged a grocery bag from the kitchen and scooped it up then rejoined the others in the living room. Dre, who was almost as good of a housekeeper as Kota, was putting the cushions back on the couch. She looked at me and shrugged. "It's the least we can do. If I were her, I wouldn't want to come home to this."

I wrapped my arms around her when she stood up. "I agree. We'll come back after we find her and clean the place up. But, right now, it's getting late and we should head to Kaitlyn's house."

Dani took the bag from me and added it to a large kitchen bag that someone must have grabbed. "We have plenty to use. It would be nice if something in here could lead us to her kidnapper."

I opened the door and climbed into the back of Phi's minivan. An inappropriate laugh escaped as I settled next to her son's football gear. Dea started laughing with me and asked, "What?"

I waved a hand in front of my face when my laughter

increased the second that I opened my mouth. "I was just thinking how the van goes from a 'soccer-mom' vehicle to a magical detective mobile. Talk about secret lives. Can you imagine what the other moms at football would say if they knew?"

That got everyone giggling as Phi headed to the Garden District. The rest of the fifteen-minute drive was spent talking about how different our lives were now. The consensus was in favor of our new magical life and all the chaos it had brought with it. I'd often wondered why things in our lives had happened the way they did. The last few weeks had convinced me that we needed to be where we were so we could help the magical world. Not many would have been able to handle what the six of us had.

Kaitlyn was in the front yard with several members of the coven when we arrived. She waved Delphine into the driveway. Dani carried the bag of Georgette's things as we greeted the head witch.

"I'm glad you reached out. Tell me what's going on. Dakota's message was cryptic," Kaitlyn said as she led us into the house.

Dea gave her a rundown of what had happened, ending with a request for help scrying for Georgette's location. The witches from outside joined us and all were gaping. A young woman with long blonde hair regarded us. "How does this stuff keep finding you six? I mean in the past two days you've faced off with Marie Leveau, worked with a *necromancer,* and are trying to find the kidnapped sister of a spirit none of us can see."

"What can we say? We're special," I replied.

Dre snorted as Dani removed each of the items from the bag and set them on the table. One second I was chuckling, and the next my vision swam with the smell of guava and blood. Dizziness made me stumble forward. Someone caught me and lowered me into a seat.

I couldn't focus on anything as the scent sucked me into a different scene. Kaitlyn's house and my sisters disappeared as a new vision came over me. This time I saw a woman in her late twenties with light brown hair and skin the exact shade of Hallie Berry's.

She was wearing clunky boots with jeans and a red top. Most notably, she was lying on a bed curled in ball while sobbing. My heart raced and my mind whirled as I tried to gather information about the room where Georgette was being held.

The bedspread was a mixture of browns while the headboard was a simple wood one. The dresser matched the bed and side table. The walls were a generic beige color, and other than that, there were no identifying characteristics. I had turned to look out the window when the door opened and a tall man with black hair and soft brown eyes walked in and headed right for the bed where he scooped Georgette into his arms and cradled her to his chest.

The scene wavered and before it disappeared, one of the mambos I recalled from the ritual to give Cami and Selene their souls back walked inside with an evil smile on her face. The guy dropped Georgette and looked like he was ready to fight.

My head throbbed and the world returned to the sound of Dani telling the others I would be alright, that I was just having a vision. "Unh, I hate coming out of those," I muttered.

Dani crouched in front of me and cradled my hands in her gloved ones. "What did you see?"

I recalled the details between sips of water that one of the witches handed me. By the end, Kaitlyn was grim faced and ready to take on Marie herself. "We need to find these mambos and stop them. Marie can claim she is unaware of their actions, but you and I know different."

Dre crossed her arms over her chest. "We need to make sure the community knows the real Marie. The less everyone fears her the less power she will have over us."

Kaitlyn gave Dre a bless-your-heart smile which was the Southern way of saying you've lost your damn mind. "Marie Leveau doesn't get her strength from our collective fear. The loa feed her, making her unbeatable."

I cleared my throat of the scratchiness that usually accompanied a vision. "All due respect Kaitlyn, but you told us yourself. Emotions hold power. I *know* fear feeds Marie. I felt it when I was in her hold. The second Kota and Dani broke through their fright and stood up to her, she didn't stick around."

Kaitlyn lifted one brow. "That wasn't some angelic heritage rearing its head?"

"It was both," Dani interjected. "I sensed when Marie started backing down and it happened right before Lia called that weird light. Regardless, can we scry for Georgette so we can stop her and her boyfriend from being attacked?"

Kaitlyn took a deep breath before letting it out. "Sure. We can discuss that more when we have our next practice session. I'll lead the ritual this time so you guys can learn how it's done."

We watched as the head witch gathered three black candles and placed them around a bowl that one of the others placed on the table. Kaitlyn picked up a silver pitcher. "This is water boiled with fennel, basil, clove, hibiscus, meadow-sweet, orange and lavender. I will help you create this to keep on hand in the event you need to scry. Having it premade allows you to get to the scrying faster."

Another witch placed a piece of paper and a pen in front of Kaitlyn. "We use the paper to write our question. After it's written, we burn it and put the ashes in the bowl. In *this* case we are going to grab some of Georgette's hair and burn it in the bowl. Burning objects yields a better result than asking the question."

When the scent of jasmine reached me, I glanced around for the source and prayed I didn't have another vision. Someone put the lit incense on the table, near the scrying set up. Kaitlyn pulled hair from the brush then set it in the bowl. With the snap of her fingers, she ignited the strands. When it went out, she poured the water over the ashes and chanted, "*Mihi quid quaero.*"

Mist filled the water before the image of Georgette floated to the surface. She was in the same bedroom I'd seen in my vision. I scanned every detail I could see to make sure I wasn't mistaken. I was so busy looking at the images in the water that I missed what Kaitlyn said next.

Whatever it was, it caused the image to shift and show the outside of a house. It looked similar to so many in New Orleans. This time the colorful house was painted red and grey. I memorized all the details I could, hoping we could later find it.

The image cleared and Kaitlyn sagged forward on the table, bracing herself on her elbows. "She's safe for now, but she is definitely struggling against an evil entity. I believe Temperance is right that the loa is trying to establish a foothold in her body and kill off her soul. I have the address for the boyfriend. Would you like help going to see him?"

Kaitlyn wrote the address on the piece of paper and handed it to Phi, who was standing closest to her. Delphine shook her head. "No, I think we have it. Lia's visions are of the future, so we shouldn't run into any problems. If that changes, we will give you a call."

Kaitlyn pursed her lips. "We're a coven, ladies. We help each other out. We are always here if you need anything."

I got up then bent next to Kaitlyn and gave her a one-armed hug. "And we appreciate it. Once we get an idea of how Georgette is, we will give you a call. If it requires witchcraft, we will need you. Tempe has agreed to help if it lies within her realm. You know, necromancers aren't all bad. She saved my life and continues to help us."

Kaitlyn gave me an odd smile before we thanked her and took our leave. Having visions tired me out and I closed my eyes after I took a seat in the back of the van. This was turning out to be much easier to solve than our last case for which I was grateful. I was seeing signs that Dea was getting back to herself. I would hate for things to take a turn for the worse and make her backslide.

CHAPTER 5

DANIELLE

*D*ea twisted the travel mug in her hand as Lia drove across town. "What the hell do I say when we see her? I'm not so sure she'll just accept that her dead sister is bugging the hell out of me because we fear a malicious loa is trying to claim her body and kill her soul."

I had to admit she had a point. It sounded insane to her and she knew it was true. Before we had witnessed magic, I never would have believed there was this unseen world complete with beings that wanted to use whoever they could for their evil machinations. Even now, I fell back into the way I thought when I was nothing more than a normal mundie. It was tough to supplant forty plus years of a certain way of thinking.

Lia threw Dea a smile. "It'd be best to leave the part about the loa out. Maybe just say her sister has a message for her? Many people believe in psychics. That won't sound so farfetched."

Dea was mid-sip when she started nodding and spilled coffee down her top. "Dammit."

I fished a tissue out of my purse and handed it to her in the backseat. "At least you're well-rested today and aren't trying to do this after coming off a double again. And you aren't alone. We'll be with you."

Dahlia chewed on her lower lip as she followed the car's directions and turned left onto a residential street. "How do we handle the danger they face from the mambos? We can't exactly say this evil voodoo practitioner is going to break into your boyfriend's place to hurt you."

The pressure on our shoulders never seemed to let up these days. It came with adventure and intrigue. I was on board with my sisters, but I'd prefer if it wasn't quite so life and death all the time.

"There's also the state of her home. I doubt she knows someone broke into it and trashed the place. We start small and keep our focus there. There's no choice but to feel our way through this as we go." I honestly saw no other way forward. It might not be smart to tell them much. That meant we would need to figure out a way to keep Georgette safe.

"And you'd better help, Giselle," Dea said to the seat next to her. Of course, to me it was empty. Although now that I paid attention, I was able to feel the slight chill in the air. It wasn't nearly as cold as I expected it to be, but it was there. "You need to find a way to stop freaking out long enough to tell me how much your sister can handle. It won't help anything if she freaks out and runs away."

"We're here," Lia announced making Dea and I look out the window. The house we'd pulled up in front of was similar to where Giselle and Georgette had lived, like so many of the duplexes in the city.

There was no use putting it off. The humidity seemed

even closer than usual, making my heart race faster and sweat instantly break out across my skin. That could have been nerves, but I couldn't say for sure because it was that muggy this morning. Without my gloves, I followed behind my sisters, letting them field the obstacles to minimize the chances of me touching anything. I couldn't wait until it was winter when it wouldn't be odd to wear them everywhere. Being thrown into memories when I touched objects was traumatic and had given me images I could never erase from my mind.

A stunning young man with green eyes and short black hair opened the door when Dea knocked. He reminded me of the plastic surgeon on Grey's Anatomy. "Can I help you?" The confusion on his face was clear. He wanted to know why three middle-aged women were standing on his doorstep.

Dea smiled and lifted a hand in a small wave. "Hi, I'm Deandra and this is my sister Dahlia and that's our sister Danielle. This is going to sound crazy, but we've come to talk to Georgette."

His eyebrows lifted into the air. "I'm Kenyon. Is she expecting you? She didn't mention anything about it."

Dea shifted from foot to foot and glanced past him. "Can we come inside? We aren't here to harm anyone, it's just an awkward conversation to have standing on your stoop."

Kenyon's eyes narrowed for a second and I was sure he would shut the door in our face, but he stood aside and gestured for us to enter. "Sure, come on in." I'm positive he was confident he could take the three of us out if we posed a threat. "Georgette might not be up to seeing you."

Dahlia gave him a supportive smile. "She's been upset and missing her sister."

"Which is why we are here. We have a message for her," Dea blurted.

We walked into a small living room that was painted

bright blue. The brown sofa seemed dull in comparison. I wondered if Kenyon was a musician given the framed posters and saxophone sitting on a stand.

Kenyon's eyes narrowed. "It's not just about her sister but about the lie her customer told about her."

I found myself copying his expression. We had no idea what he was talking about and couldn't play along. Dea saved us from having to when she explained a little more about why we were there. "We went to Blade first, but were told she wasn't working at the salon anymore. That she had quit. You see, I'm a psychic and her sister has come to me asking that I find Georgette."

Kenyon's expression transformed into a scowl. "This isn't funny. I'm not going to allow you to prey on Georgette. She's been through enough as it is."

"It's okay, Ken. I can see through lies well-enough. I just wish Peggy was able to, as well. If she had seen that woman's falsities, I would still have a job." Georgette was standing in the open doorway to what I assumed was the bedroom. In shotgun houses you walked straight through each room to reach the back of the house.

There were dark circles under her red, puffy eyes and her hair looked like it hadn't been brushed for a few days. "You can deliver Giselle's message and leave." The tremor in her voice broke my heart.

Dea took a step towards her but stopped when Kenyon moved into her path. "It's not as simple as delivering the message. Communication with her spirit is difficult."

Georgette stepped up to Kenyon who put his arm around her. I noted her entire body was trembling. "Are you telling me you need to do a séance for me to talk to Giselle?"

Dea shot Lia and me wide eyes. I dipped my head telling her to go with it. Dea turned to face the couple again. "Sorry, I'm new to this and rely on my sisters for support." I wasn't sure why she said that but it helped put Georgette at ease. "Doing a séance would certainly make talking to Giselle easier. Although, I can't guarantee you will understand all of what she wants me to tell you."

Tears filled Georgette's eyes. "I'd love to talk to her again, in any way I can. We used to rely on each other, too. My life has fallen apart since Gisi died. If it wasn't for Kenyon, I'm not sure where I would be. He let me stay with him despite the fact that we'd only been on a couple of dates. I couldn't go home after I lost my job. It was too hard. I felt like I failed Giselle."

That broke the dam holding back her tears and they started falling down her cheeks. Georgette was strong though and despite the emotional pain, she kept herself on her feet. "So, how do we do this? Do you need candles, or a crystal ball or something?"

Dea shook her head from side to side making me wonder what the hell she was thinking. We had to do something showy or she would never believe us. That's how mundies thought it worked.

"There are candles and things involved but I didn't bring them with me. I wasn't sure how you would react. And I know this sounds crazy, believe me. We own the Willow-berry Plantation, and I would appreciate it if you could follow us out there so we can contact your sister." Dea was talking fast and wringing her hands and completely uncertain.

I worried they would balk, calling us nut bags. In the end Georgette related to her disquiet. "This must be hard for you to have stranger ghosts coming to you asking to contact their families."

Dea chuckled as she nodded. "You have no idea. Never in my life did I think I would be doing something like this. I'm a nurse at the hospital full-time and didn't used to see spirits that often but I couldn't ignore your sister. She wouldn't let me."

Kenyon stared at us with undisguised distrust. "Georgette doesn't have money that you can milk from her if that's your angle."

Dea's hands went in the air palms out. "That isn't our angle at all. I'm not asking her to pay me for this in any way. I have honestly been compelled by Giselle to contact her. That's it, nothing more."

"So, this isn't going to cost anything and you're doing this at a plantation where the public comes and goes?" Georgette was still trembling, despite the fact that she had moved away from Kenyon and was standing on her own now.

"That's right," Dea replied as she lowered her hands.

"Alright. We will meet you there. If I'm leaving the house I'd like to shower," Georgette replied.

We gave them the address and left. Deandra pulled out her phone and started typing into the search bar. "What the hell do I do for a séance? What the hell was I thinking? I'm not some crystal ball gazing phony."

I couldn't help it as a laugh bubbled out of me. Dea and Lia joined in and the three of us were laughing when I told Lia to stop by Solid Solutions. "We can pick up a crystal ball and ask Hollie what she knows about seances."

Dea shook her head. "You two get the crystal, I'm calling Tempe. She's far more likely to have the information for me. I also plan to ask how she managed to calm Giselle down. I need to be able to communicate with her. Georgette will no doubt have questions to verify credibility."

"That's probably a better plan. As long as you can communicate with Giselle, the rest won't matter." I liked the fact that Dea's idea would give her more information on how to work with ghosts.

Given where Kenyon lived, Lia was pulling up to Solid

Solutions and we were jumping out of the car before we knew it. The tinkle of the bell above the door and the same smell of incense greeted us as the last time we had been in.

Hollie came out from the back wearing a pair of black camo leggings and a coral-colored crop top. "Danielle, Dahlia! So good to see you. What brings you back so soon?"

Dahlia touched the crystal ball on top of the glass display case. "We need a crystal ball for our sister Deandra. She's going to do a séance for a customer."

Hollie's forehead furrowed and her lips pursed. "She's the one with necromancer powers, right?"

I nodded. "Yes, why? Do you discriminate against necromancers?"

Hollie's eyes widened and her head shook from side to side. "Not at all. It's just that this particular crystal sphere is for tourists. The ones below the glass are the ones that will actually enhance her power and help her channel her energy making it easier to communicate with the spirits. Temperance, one of the local necromancers has vouched that they work as advertised."

Lia and I both shrugged before Lia reached for the company credit card. "That's precisely what she will need. Dea is actually talking to Tempe out in the car."

I pointed to the stand beneath the orb, "Does it come with the brass stand? She should have that. Not to mention it'll become part of the décor for our magical kitchen, and I love the ornate curls of the legs."

Hollie laughed. "It does come with it. I prefer the brass and silver stands to the wood ones, so I don't carry them."

The witch rung us up and we were out the door within minutes. Dea was chewing on her lower lip when we got in the car. I handed her the bag. "Was she able to help?"

Dea peered in the paper bag. "Yeah. She gave me a spell to open communication and get rid of the noise interfering with Gisele's focus. She also gave me a spell to use to purge the loa from Georgette. She said it would likely be my only chance to force it out of the young woman and I shouldn't let it pass."

Lia looked over her shoulder as she made her way back to Willowberry. "And you're terrified over the prospect. It sounds scary as hell, but keep in mind spirits are your thing. You can do this. And we will all be right there to support you."

Dea put her head in her hands. "Maliko would freak the hell out if he knew I was going to put on this show and then kick a god out of someone's body."

"It's not something he needs to know. You are going to be fine. You should cast a protection spell over yourself before you start to be sure," I told her.

She nodded and released a sigh as she lifted her head. "That's probably smart. I'll feel better if I do."

"Which will make you more confident. That will impact your intent making a huge difference when doing the spell," Lia added.

Dea was lost in her head the rest of the drive and neither Lia nor I pushed her to talk. We left her to whatever she was thinking. I texted Kota and Dre and asked them to set up a table with our new silk cloth in the women's parlor for a ritual.

By the time we reached Willowberry, Georgette and Kenyon were already there talking to Dre and Kota in the parlor. "You guys made it here fast," Dea said by way of greeting. "Are you ready for this, Georgette? It's going to be emotional for you, I'm sure."

Dre and Kota had created a legitimate looking psychic space. The small round table had the silk cloth with candles lit on top of it. They'd also added a cauldron to the book case along one wall. Several of the jars of herbs lined the mantle above the fireplace and the ceramic palm was front and center.

Georgette trembled as she turned in a circle. "Ready as I'll ever be."

I grabbed the bag from Dea and stepped away when her back was to me. As surreptitiously as possible, I removed the base and crystal ball. It wasn't until I had the set in my hand that I realized I didn't have my gloves on. Thankfully the items were new and didn't have any memories attached to them, yet.

I set them in the center of the table then stepped to the side of the room. After grabbing a third chair for the table, Lia, Dre, and Kota joined me. The four of us remained silent as Dea gestured to the chairs. "Have a seat."

Dea sat down and took a deep breath. "I'm going to call to Giselle. When she joins us, I'll tell you what she wants you to know. I'm not sure how long I will be able to hold her here, so there might not be time for questions."

Georgette's eyes filled with tears as she nodded. "I just want to know if she's okay."

Dea inclined her head then placed her palms around the clear crystal ball. "*Aperiam communicationis et purgare chao.*"

Air whipped through the room, blowing my hair across my eyes. Georgette gasped while Kenyon scanned the room most likely looking for a fan. I was too busy taking in the cool feel of Dea's magic. It made my skin prickle and tingle at the same time. Meanwhile the crystal ball went from clear to the bluish glow of a ghost. It was eerie as hell because I knew it was powered by a spirit.

Dea opened her eyes and focused on a spot to the side of Georgette. "She's here and she wants me to start by saying she's better now that she can talk to you."

Georgette turned to look where Dea was. "I miss you. I feel like I can't breathe most days."

"Giselle says it's time to suck it up and put on your dancing shoes because your party is only just beginning. Especially, with a smokin' guy like Kenyon." Dea was smiling as she relayed the message.

Georgette gasped and her hand flew to her mouth. "It really is her. No one knew we used to say that to one another. Oh my, God." The tears fell down her cheeks and she hunched in on herself.

Dea kept her hands on the crystal and her gaze on Georgette. "Your sister needs you to know that you have to stay strong. Your life depends on it. If you allow the grief to take over, you will lose yourself to an evil entity. You have a great guy that seems to like you a lot. Don't let them win."

Georgette moved closer to Kenyon and nodded. "I can try. Can you ask her if she knows what happened to her?"

Dea shook her head from side to side. "She said it happened too fast and didn't see much. I'd like to try something I think will make you feel better."

At Georgette's nod, Dea chanted, *"Purgate deum."*

Georgette started shaking and whimpering. Kenyon drew her close and glared daggers at Dea. If looks could kill, she would be dead at the moment. Georgette jerked in his arms and Dea jumped up, circling around the table. I was at their side in an instant, as were Lia, Dre and Kota.

"What's happening to her?" Kenyon asked.

Dea shook her head. "I'm not certain but I think she's battling her, uh grief. Just remind her to be strong."

Kenyon bent his mouth to Georgette's ear and started murmuring that she needed to hang on so they could go on more dates. It seemed to take forever, but it was more like a couple of minutes before Georgette lifted her head. "How would you feel about taking a trip to New York City with me? Giselle and I planned on going next year."

Kenyon laughed and held her close. "It's a date. Are you alright?"

Georgette smiled at him and nodded. "I think I'm going to be alright."

I jumped when the lights flickered and thunder rumbled. Lia and I shared a look before I saw the same wide-eyed fear in Dre and Kota's face. How the hell was Dea doing that? I was ninety percent certain that Dea had just banished the loa. Was it having a hissy fit as it was being pushed out?

My thoughts splintered as several things happened at once. Georgette smiled and thanked Dea giving her a hug. Georgette said something about being able to move on now that she'd heard from her sister one more time. Georgette and Kenyon left with Georgette having a bounce in her step that had been missing before. As the thunder continued outside, I felt something punch through me. It felt like I'd gotten a fishhook through my lungs.

Afraid something had gone wrong I probed around, searching for my magic and anything that might be amiss. I shook off the sensation and immediately felt foolish for being afraid the loa had hurt me in some way.

Dea was bent over blowing out the candles on the table. "Giselle is leaving with her sister. She says she isn't ready to move on and that she wants to look over Georgette to make sure she doesn't allow herself to wither just because she is gone."

I was surprised Dea wasn't happier about the outcome. She'd accomplished something major. She should be beaming from ear to ear and dancing a jig.

Lia was smiling enough for the both of them. "I can't believe how easy that was to resolve. And how fast we were able to find Georgette and take care of it."

I snorted. "That's what happens when you have more

information than a description that could apply to thousands of people."

Everyone laughed at that while Lia stuck her tongue out at me. "This deserves a cupcake to celebrate."

I couldn't agree more. A sweet treat was precisely what I needed to banish the lingering creepy feeling. We'd helped a pair of sisters and had a second line parade to finish planning.

CHAPTER 6

❦

DAHLIA

*M*y hands shook as Lucas twined his fingers through mine. It had been years since I'd gone on a date with a guy. At some point I gave up on thinking about ever having anyone else in my life. I was content with how things were. Until Lucas. He came along and upended things in a messy but nice way. Now, I found myself dating a sexy shifter. "Are you alright? I thought you said Dea banished the loa easily this afternoon. We can return to Willowberry if you'd rather not go out."

I smiled up at him, taking in his earnest grey eyes that were slightly obscured by a lock of his brown hair falling over his forehead. "I want to be here with you. I was just thinking about how odd it feels to be dating again. It's been a long time for me."

He opened the door to Silver Hound, a restaurant owned by an alligator shifter named Jack. Dani said the food was phenomenal. The restaurant was one of the few places paranormals could go without fear of being outed and given the way things had been going lately, I thought that was safest.

Lucas bent and pressed his lips to mine. "It's been a while for me, too. We've gotten to know each other pretty well over the past few months but I still find that I'm nervous."

The tension riding me lessened hearing him admit that he was just as uncertain. It made him a little more real to me. There were times I would look at him and think he must be one of my visions, that he couldn't be real. He was just too perfect.

I chuckled. "That's a relief to hear. As long as zombies don't attack the restaurant and I don't have a vision, we'll have a great time." I prayed nothing interfered with our night. I'd been dreaming of Lucas more nights than not, and I was ready to take things to the next level, even if the thought gave me butterflies.

My thoughts fractured when Lucas stopped at a door that had a weathered name painted on the dingy window. I stumbled as Lucas tugged me inside and we were greeted by a huge guy, rather than a young woman or man like I expected. The guy could easily be six and a half feet tall with muscles upon muscles bulging under his blue flannel shirt. He had flawless dark brown skin and warm black irises.

"Jack," Lucas called out as they clasped forearms. "Good to see you, man."

This was the guy that sent Nedasea our way. Jack clapped Lucas's back and they released each other. "It's good to see you. This must be one of the Twisted Sisters."

My mouth parted slightly before I caught my reaction and closed it. "Yes, I'm Dahlia. Nice to meet you. Thanks for spreading the word about us."

"Trust me. It's my pleasure. You're helping me more than you know. There aren't many places for people to throw parties and they used to come here, but I hate closing to the public to host one," Jack admitted. "C'mon, let's get you guys to a table. I have some fresh blackened mahi mahi tonight if you're interested. It's served with dirty rice and broccoli."

Lucas nudged the base of my spine for me to go first. I followed the alligator shifter through a space with gray walls and black tables and chairs. The place would have been ordinary if not for the one-foot-tall man that was the same shade as the rust-colored floor. And then there were the pixies sitting at a table made for a doll house. Next to them was a couple that looked like mundies until they turned and you saw their pointed ears and wings.

Jack took our drink order and by the time he returned we both ordered dinner. I got the special. I loved mahi mahi and couldn't wait to eat. Lucas ordered red beans and rice, a steak and the fried green tomato appetizer.

"These are the only tomatoes I eat," I admitted when a young woman with horns curling around the side of her head delivered the first round.

Lucas gasped and clutched his chest. "How did I not know this? I feel like we don't even know each other."

I sighed as if I was put out. "I should have led with that. I tend to keep that hidden because it causes so much drama. Oh well, it wasn't a total loss. I got to make out with a sexy wolf. I can mark that off my bucket list."

Lucas threw back his head and laughed as I cut a piece of the fried goodness and dipped it in the spicy sauce. A moan left my mouth as flavors burst across my tongue. "Holy shit that sauce is delicious. Jack should bottle and sell that shit."

Lucas's gray eyes darkened as he watched me eat another bite. Heat spread through my veins as I fought the urge to forgo dinner and drag him back to my bed. I'd never had a guy look at me the way Lucas did and wondered if it was a shifter thing. I swear he looked like he was ready to eat me up. In the best way possible.

Jack delivered our cocktails, interrupting the moment. "I've actually thought about bottling the sauce, but I'd need to use preservatives and that'll change the flavor."

I blinked and shook my head to clear it. What had he said? He was still standing at the side of our table. Oh, right the sauce. "Changing the flavor would be a crime. You could always sell what you have left at the end of the night, assuming it'll last people a couple of days. You'd make money and minimize waste."

"Spoken like a true businesswoman. I like it. I usually toss a good amount every few days. I'll have to think about it. Thanks." Jack tapped the side of the table and walked away.

The horned waitress delivered our food and as we ate, we talked about other foods we liked and didn't. It was fun to tease him about not liking okra. That was sacrilegious in my book given it was the key ingredient in gumbo, one of my favorites. Not to mention it was delicious fried and sauteed.

Lucas paid for our meal and we were back outside where the evening had cooled from the heat of the afternoon. I grabbed his hand and tugged him close. "Would you like to take a walk to digest some of this food? I'll fall into a food coma if I sit down right now."

He ran a finger over my cheek. "I'd love to. As long as we avoid the drunk tourists on Bourbon."

I rolled my eyes and started walking toward Jackson Square. "You couldn't pay me to go down there right now."

We walked in silence for a few seconds before Lucas tugged me down the alley next to the St. Louis Cathedral. I was stunned by the move and didn't process what he was doing until he pressed me up against the side of the building next to the church.

I felt every inch of his long, lean body against mine. He cupped my cheek with one hand and grabbed my ass with the other. His lips descended on mine at the same time he pulled my groin into the erection straining his pants.

He kissed me like his life depended on it. Desire burned through me like a wildfire along the California coast. My hands went to his chest where my nails dug into him through his t-shirt.

I was pretty sure he would have stripped me naked if we hadn't heard shouting. Lucas turned with a snarl and too many teeth. I prayed we weren't dealing with a drunken mundie.

My mind blanked for several seconds when I caught sight of the guy pointing a stick at Lucas and me. "What's going on?" The guy was dressed in a dark purple, almost black jacket with feathers around the lapels and he had a top hat on with a feather sticking out of the side. There were others behind him, as well, only they were dressed in normal jeans and t-shirts.

"Something's off with that mundie. He feels different to me." Lucas held me behind his body.

My hands curled into fists on his back as my mind rifled through possible spells I could use. "What do you mean?"

"I'm not sure. Can you do a reveal spell?"

That was an easy one. I didn't hesitate to focus my intent on revealing their true nature before I chanted, "*Revelare.*"

My magic flowed out of me and moved in their direction. I saw the second it hit the guy. He growled low and moved closer to us at the same time the air wavered around him like a mirage. When I tilted my head, I caught sight of something that chilled my blood. When Giselle came to us, I started researching the loa to gather all of the information I could on the voodoo deities.

If I wasn't mistaken, this man was indeed possessed. "He's got Baron Samedi running the show."

Lucas looked over his shoulder with a furrowed brow. *"What?"*

"Samedi is a loa. He's fond of rum, tobacco and cursing." My focus shifted to the loa approaching us. It wasn't a mundie after all. It was the god in spirit form.

As he got closer, I could see he wasn't corporeal after all. And the people behind him followed along with him. I hadn't given them a second look but somehow Samedi was controlling them because they all glowed with the same dark purple light that emanated off the god.

Lucas cursed as he turned around and lifted his hands into the air. His fingers were tipped with claws. "How do I fight a spirit? We need to get out of here."

That seemed to piss Samedi off and he closed the distance. I cast a hasty protection spell. It managed to stop the loa while I wracked my brain for everything that I'd learned about him.

Baron Samedi was the leader of the Guédé family of loa, and was the loa of graveyards, gravestones, and resurrection. His description on the internet was spot on, down to the skull-like face. Perhaps his face was a skull. It was difficult to tell for sure. There was nothing about how we could defeat the god.

While I stood there recalling everything I'd learned, I felt something vile latch onto me. I'd never given much thought to whether or not I had a soul until that moment because I swear something hooked right through it.

My chest tightened and my heart started racing. I grabbed for Lucas, gasping for air. Thankfully, Lucas didn't need to be told precisely what was happening. He picked me up and took off further down the alley away from the god.

I discovered very quickly that distance didn't matter and hit Lucas to make him stop. He paused before we moved out into the open area of Jackson Square. My gaze fell on the well-lit garden behind the wrought iron fence and the people milling around the area. They were tourists that had no idea danger lurked a few feet away.

Lucas lifted my gaze to his. "What is it? How can I help?"

I sucked in what air I could get past the constriction in my throat. "I'm not sure. I need to think."

The only thought that kept racing through my mind was this fucker needed to go or who knew what he would do with my soul and my body. "He's trying to push his way inside and take over. He wants me for some reason."

Lucas's eyes looked like a stormy day at sea as he clenched his jaw so tight that I heard a crack. "How do we stop it? I know you don't need to be told how bad that would be for you."

My eyes filled with tears of frustration as my mind remained blank. "You're a witch and fae, love. You can force the energy out of your body."

I thought about what he said. "Okay, I can do this." My chest hurt from the pressure, making it hard to think straight. "Can you look up 'you have no right to my soul, be gone' in Latin?" It wasn't very eloquent but it was the best I could manage under the circumstances.

Lucas pulled out his phone and typed into the search engine. Samedi was casually walking down the alley toward us with his entourage in tow. Lucas held the phone out to me with the result for my spell.

I concentrated on forcing the loa from my body and closed him out with a solid iron barrier. With that firmly focused in my mind, I chanted, *"Non habetis ad animam meam, abiit."*

Samedi opened his mouth and shrieked loud enough to rattle the windows of the church next to us. He pointed his walking stick at us before he vanished in a puff of smoke.

The pressure in my chest vanished so quickly that I sagged forward.

Thankfully Lucas caught me because the smell of rotten eggs made my head swim and the alley vanished, along with Lucas and the people that had been under Samedi's influence.

In its place I saw a mambo dressed in the dark red ceremonial cloak holding one of their carved sticks. I recognized her from the ritual, but she wasn't the same one that barged into Kenyon's house. The mambo lifted a knife in her other hand and chanted something in a foreign language. Her focus dropped and I caught sight of a young woman lying on a stone table. The mambo brought the knife down and stabbed her.

A scream bubbled up in my throat as I watched the mambo dance around the table while the young woman's blood dripped into bowls set on the floor. I shifted my gaze hoping to see where they were and saw a room filled with symbols, black candles and chicken parts. Oh, and the loa Baron Samedi.

Samedi took possession of the woman's body. The young woman jerked upright and had glowing red eyes while power sparked from her fingertips. The scene vanished as abruptly as it began.

I returned to warm arms cradling me against a hard chest. My head was pounding and my energy was gone. Lucas pressed his lips to mine briefly. "What did you see?"

I recounted the events and asked him to put me down. He set me on my feet but didn't release me. "What do I do? How do we find this mambo and stop her? This is so much worse than watching the skin walker kill an innocent woman."

Lucas nudged me into moving. It was then that I noticed the people were already at the other end of the alley looking around with confused expressions.

"We stop this mambo. I don't know how yet, but you're the only one that can." Lucas's belief in me warmed my heart. There wasn't even the hint of doubt and indecision that I experienced.

My stomach twisted into knots as my mind went back to my encounter with Marie Leveau outside Solid Solutions. There was no way I would ever set one foot in Marie's territory and risk pissing her off. I respected her power and ability to hurt me and those I loved, so we had better find a way around that.

CHAPTER 7

DANIELLE

The parasol was blurred as my hand traced its glittered fleur-de-lis pattern. We had fifty to make for Ava's family. Part of what we offered our clients was custom accessories for their events. It was something the six of us proudly did by hand or using one of our machines. Sadly, we didn't have one that could do things like this which left us to painstakingly add such details as glitter.

Dre growled and set her bottle of glitter paint down with exaggerated care. "I can't do the designs. My hands aren't steady enough and I am not patient enough to make them look as good as you guys. I'll add the fringe around the edges then I can work on Ava's sash and the large feather fans."

Phi chuckled as she smiled at our sister. "You and Lia both. I'm certain the reason she agreed to go out on that date with Lucas was to avoid doing these with us."

Knowing our strengths and weaknesses was the reason we worked so well with one another. Dre and Lia were the worker bees of our group and the first to dig into a laborious task. Phi and I were right there with them but much better suited to the fine details of any project. Kota usually chose the easy route in all things and Dea was universal and could do just about anything we needed.

I got up to stretch and hang the finished parasol upside down on the line to dry the added symbols. "Whatever we do, we can't tease her about going out with Lucas. You know we've been telling her for years to start dating. We don't want to spook her, now."

Dre rolled her eyes. "We may have believed she was ready before. Most people would have moved on long before she did, but we weren't in her shoes. It's easy to say what we would have done but our husbands weren't violently murdered. Besides, Lucas is a good guy and well worth the wait."

Cami came into the barn carrying a tray of drinks. "Wow, you guys work fast. How did you get four more done? I wasn't gone that long."

I picked up one of the parasols and twirled it. "We have only finished the fleur-de-lis on these. They have to dry completely before we draw on the other sections."

Cami set the tray down. "You say that like the amount you managed isn't significant."

Phi and Dre snorted making me scowl at them. "There's still a lot to do, so I don't get caught up in what was done until it's all done."

"And that won't be until we are leaving for the Quarter for the parade, seeing as there are always last-minute projects," Cami observed.

Dre chuckled at that. "Dani always finds things to add right before an event happens. It's what makes these fun and frustrating at the same time."

The door opened again, and Dahlia walked in with Lucas

in tow. Lia's face was pinched and her expression haunted. I replaced the parasol and rushed to her side. "What happened? What did you see this time? Not another murder, I hope."

Lucas squeezed Lia to his side. "After dinner we had an encounter with Samedi then she had a vision."

I gestured them inside the barn where we were working. "My smell-o-vision showed me a horrific sight of the same mambo sacrificing a woman for the loa."

Dre joined us and waved a hand through the air. "Wait, a minute. Back up. What was this encounter with Baron Samedi? I thought he was banished from this realm."

Lia sucked in a shuddering breath. "We all thought that's what happened, but we were wrong. He tried to attach to my soul. I felt this tug followed by his presence pushing his way inside. I was forced to push him away with a spell."

My mind raced to recall everything we'd learned while researching the loa. It was impossible to know which of the details were accurate and which were false when reading shit on the internet. I thought it said somewhere that the loa couldn't remain in our reality for long without a host. "How is that even possible? The ritual to put Selene and Cami's souls back inside their bodies was months ago. Shouldn't he be back in his realm, or whatever?"

Lia lifted one shoulder. "My best guess is that Samedi keeps burning through his hosts. Mundies aren't powerful enough and I'd bet money he can't just jump inside a paranormal and take the wheel."

"There's no doubt about that. Marie's attempt to hijack the soul ritual is proof enough of the latter at least." Dre pulled her phone out of her back pocket. "We need to contact Dea and see if she's experienced anything else from the spirit realm and see what she suggests."

"Hello, sestra. What's going on, is everything okay?" Dea's

voice was tense when she answered rather than her typical upbeat greeting.

Lia explained what had happened and Dre finished by asking what she thought we should do.

The sound of a heart monitor echoed through the cell phone speaker while Deandra either considered the question or took vitals before she could respond. It was a few seconds before she came back on the line. "Sorry about that, I had to give a patient some meds. As much as I hate to even suggest this, the best course of action will be to pay Marie Leveau a visit and ask her about the events of the evening. First, I want to see if she is surrounded by souls. And second, I want to gauge her reaction to the idea that one of her mambos might be acting against her orders. That's really the only way we will know if she is behind this. Not to mention, if she isn't, she can help us locate the offending mambo."

My gut twisted into a sailor's knot. "There's no way we should go into her lair to ask her about the vision and the loa."

Deandra sighed. "My shift just ended. I'll stop by on my way home and we can discuss this more."

My forehead furrowed. "What do you mean it just ended. You're scheduled until seven in the morning, right?" It was barely eleven at night, she should be there eight more hours.

Dea didn't respond to that question as the line went dead. I looked at the phone in Dreya's hand. "What the heck was that? Do you think she called off early?"

Phi shrugged her shoulders. "She must have. Nothing else makes sense. Even if you're a part-time employee they have you on twelve-hour shifts."

Lucas watched Dahlia as she stepped away from him. "Why is this important? After the week she's had, I imagine she needs a break from the stress of the hospital."

Lia's expression turned incredulous. "You've never had to

worry about paying your bills, have you? We grew up having our water or electricity shut off because our parents couldn't pay a bill. They worked their asses off but when you had ten children, money only went so far. It's why we all work our tails off to make our business successful. And why Dea and Phi still work outside the Six Twisted Sisters."

Lucas's eyes widened and his mouth parted in obvious shock. "I didn't grow up privileged but my parents didn't struggle like that, either. With the pack living on pack land and pooling our resources together, we are able to build houses without having to take out loans. It's much easier to pay taxes when there are many putting in to cover the bill. Much like I imagine the plantation being for your family eventually."

I had to admit the idea was appealing on some level. There was enough land to build new houses and plenty of existing structures that could be renovated. "I'm not sure that anyone else will move here."

Dre lifted a shoulder. "The brothers won't want to live so close. Maybe some of the kids. None of that is the point. Taking time off isn't like Dea. We've been bugging her not to work so many doubles. They take a huge toll on you."

"Days that we've worked eighteen or more hours, I can barely keep my eyes open by the time I get home," Lucas admitted. "We can wait to hear her side of things, but I will caution you guys against paying Marie a visit. She's notoriously vicious and never answers to anyone. Word on the street is that you six have challenged her. She won't like that."

Lia winced and dropped her head. Because Lucas was watching her like a hawk, he noticed. "What happened? What haven't you told me?"

No one said anything. This was Lia's news to share or not. It didn't take long for Dahlia to give Lucas a rundown of the encounter with Marie Leveau outside of Solid Solutions.

By the time she was done, Lucas was frowning and bristling with agitated energy.

Lucas grabbed Lia's shoulders and held her in front of him. "You make it difficult to ever want to leave your side. Next time tell me right away when something like this happens."

Knowing my sister had an independent streak a mile wide, I wasn't surprised when Lia bristled and jerked out of his hold. "Someone is living in the dark ages still. I'm not your property. Nor am I helpless. Not telling you went against what we talked about before and I know I've gotten in over my head. However, I wasn't alone and I know better than to allow that to happen if I can help it. I told you I would never knowingly walk into danger, but I will not allow Marie to think she can intimidate me. Part of her power comes from the fear others have of her. She won't get that from me."

Lucas pressed his forehead to hers and took a deep breath. "You're right. That didn't come out right. I'm asking you to call me. You're one of the most courageous women I know. You and your sisters are the talk of the magical community for many reasons. Most appreciate what is being said, but others are angry about it and that puts a target on your backs. I'd like to be a part of protecting your very fine ass."

Dahlia squeaked and jumped away from Lucas making him laugh. She shook her head at him with her cheeks turning pinker by the second. "Keeping this from you wasn't intentional. I had planned on telling you after dinner. I wanted a meal without all of this drama. I wouldn't change that for the world, even if you do like tomatoes. The encounter with Samedi sidetracked me afterwards."

"What about the loa?" Dea asked as she walked into the room.

Everyone's attention shifted to Deandra. The knot in my gut worsened when I caught sight of the flat expression on her face. She'd been back to herself right after helping the twins. Now she seemed right back where she had been before.

"Just talking about what happened," Lia answered then gave Dea a rundown of what had happened.

Dea leaned against the table, grabbed the tall-boy off the tray and cracked it open. All eyes widened as we watched her drink the Pepsi. She usually never drank the soda. She must be really tired. "I stand by my assessment that we need to go to Marie Leveau."

The suggestion didn't sit any better with me. "Why do you say that?"

Dea poured some of the pop into the cup of ice and handed it to me. "Because she's got power over her mambos and could make sure Lia's vision doesn't happen. It would save us trying to hunt this woman down to try and stop her. Have you forgotten our motto of work smarter not harder?"

I rolled my eyes. "Please. I'm the queen of making things harder for us. It's what we thrive on." Yes, I lived in my delusional world where my sisters enjoyed the same level of chaos that I did.

"Which is a thing of the past now that we are doing this full-time," Dre clarified. "Without your focus being split in five million different directions at home and the hospital, events have gotten easier to plan and prepare for. As for paying Marie a visit, I'm not so sure that's the wisest plan. Why don't we ask to meet her in neutral territory?"

Deandra said something about wanting to see the Queen of Voodoo in her natural habitat so she was able to determine if there are spirits tethered to her. I only half listened to how a practitioner of death magic could attach souls to bodies when they were behind their demise because Lia pulled me aside.

Lia stood right next to me, so no one else would hear what she said. "What is wrong with Dea? Are you buying this need to search for spirits and go to Leveau's lair?"

I considered what she was asking. Our lives had been turned upside down a few months ago, when Phoebe unlocked our dormant DNA, igniting our magical genes. The magical world was beyond anything we'd been expecting, or were prepared for.

"I have no idea what's going through Dea's head. We both know that she's burning the candle at both ends. Between the night shift at the hospital and helping us during the day when she can, she doesn't have much down time. If she pulls a double, it's even worse for her. And that doesn't include her being awake for Mateo when he gets home from school." I kept my voice to a whisper like Lia had.

Dahlia's hand went to her chest where she rubbed circles over her heart. "Perhaps we should have her do less here. That's enough to wear anyone out. The last thing we need is for her powers to get out of her control."

Kaitlyn had explained that our magic was far more likely to misfire or act beyond our ability to control the more fatigued we became. She'd painted a pretty compelling picture that we should have taken seriously, but we'd grown up working to help support the family, so stretching ourselves was second nature.

Phi held up her hands. "Whoa, Dea. I get that you want to get a better measure of the Voodoo Queen. I have two words to say to that. Zombie attack. Have you forgotten about the dead ravaging the plantation and coming after us? If it wasn't for the pixies, Lia would be fighting flesh eating bacteria as we speak."

Deandra shrugged her shoulders. "That was a night I will

never forget. What you guys are pushing aside is the fact that we have skills and powerful allies that will be here to help us when needed. We can't put Marie in her place if we don't understand the power she has taken from others. The only way we will get an idea is to show up at her place unexpected. She dons a mask when given the time."

Dahlia crossed her arms over her chest. "We should table this discussion. We shouldn't make a move until we train more with Kaitlyn. She's coming tomorrow. That'll also give you time to get some much-needed rest, Dea."

Sleep sounded like a good plan for everyone. It was late and we'd been working all evening without a break. Dahlia's date ended with a traumatic encounter with a loa and Dea was still off. I was happy to leave these considerations for tomorrow. If I was lucky, a good night's sleep would give all of us a clearer head.

CHAPTER 8

DAHLIA

"*H*ello, Dahlia," Talewen called out as she flew out of the new grove of trees at the edge of the plantation. Her long blue hair was loose and blew behind her like the streamers on the handlebars of a bicycle. "Are you guys practicing today?"

I lifted a hand to the pixie. "We're going to be making potions today. Given everything we've gone through, Kaitlyn thinks we need to have a basic grasp, so we can create something if the need arises."

Talewen flew beside me as I continued to the building we'd selected for our magical kitchen. The structure had been a shed used to store the various equipment needed for the plantation. Lucas and Noah had reinforced the walls and made sure the roof was sound. The interior had shelving units and tables with stools but the walls were unfinished, and there was no air conditioning in the place. It was going to be difficult to stay cool with all the burners heating our cauldrons, but it was the best location we had.

My eyes widened when I laid my eyes on what looked like it was going to be a greenhouse built next to the magical kitchen. "What's that?"

Talewen's cheeks tinged pink as she zipped forward to greet the other pixies in her mound. "We wanted to surprise you with this. It isn't quite done yet and it's smaller than you might want, but it's a start," Talewen said as she, Ceisella, Jelin, Adern and Janoac hovered in front of the glass and wood structure.

I paused at one corner and crouched to look at the wood base of the walls. It looked like they'd used reclaimed wood for the thing. The roof was made of wood with skylights. There was no glass as of yet, but I saw the planting beds built inside already.

Standing up, I smiled at the tiny creatures. "This is unreal. We never expected anything like this. We planned on using the garden to grow what herbs we would need. Dre has a green thumb, but Dani and I don't. The last succulent I had died on me."

Ceisella giggled and flew in a circle. "We will help maintain the space. As you know, some of us enjoy using our earth magic to care for the plants. Lucas and Noah are procuring the frosted glass we will need for it, so it could be some time before we are ready to plant anything."

I inclined my head. "I know I speak for my sisters when I say that you didn't need to do this. Although, I know they will appreciate it as much as I do. We'd planned on buying the herbs we need from Solid Solutions. This is far more convenient. I need to set up for potions practice but I won't say anything to my sisters so you can appreciate their surprise."

Talewen and Ceisella followed me as I went to the kitchen a few feet away. Like the greenhouse outside, the place wasn't very big. And I got my second surprise of the day when I walked inside and noticed the space was finished. At some point, Lucas and Noah had hung drywall and painted the walls.

I crossed to the shelves and grabbed one of the cauldrons and its stand then placed it in front of one of the stools. Talewen and Ceisella helped without me asking and before long we had seven stations set up and the jars of herbs placed around each one.

The door opened and I turned, expecting to see Dani and Dre, but it was Lucas and Noah. Lucas crossed the room and scooped me up into his arms. I opened my mouth to ask what he was doing when he pressed his lips to mine. The kiss was brief, but heated, and left me yearning for more from him.

Our date the night before hadn't ended how I'd hoped. I'd gone from being ready for more with him to having to ward off a loa's assault. Not exactly something to keep me in a sexy mood.

"What are you doing here?" I asked when he let me up for air.

His smile melted my heart. "We came to paint the outside, to protect the wood, when I smelled your scent. I couldn't resist coming in for a kiss."

Heat suffused my cheeks as I ran my hands over his shoulders. "Well, it's certainly a nice surprise. Thanks for getting the inside finished. Kota and Dani will no doubt want to finish decorating the place after practice. Oh, and thanks for helping the pixies with the greenhouse. You, too, Noah."

Lucas looked over at Ceisella and Talewen, giving them a nod. "They did all the work. They even located the wood they used. All we did was loan them some tools and offered to pick up some glass for them."

Noah lifted one shoulder. "It's our pleasure. Where's your beautiful sister?"

I gestured in the direction of the main house. "She's likely on her way over in the golf cart by now."

A grin spread across Noah's face before he turned and loped out the door. The pixies followed suit, with Lucas and I following at a slower pace. "I'm sorry our date got interrupted last night. That isn't how I imagined it ending." I clamped my mouth shut as a can of worms wiggled in my stomach. I hadn't meant to say so much.

Lucas twined his fingers with mine. "Then it's a good thing I have another one planned if you're up for it."

My smile probably made me look like a loon, but I couldn't dial it back. "As long as it isn't anywhere that we might run into the loa. I want a normal date without interruptions."

Lucas laughed at that, and the sound rumbled over me, making me want things from him that I hadn't thought about in far too long. "That's not a thing where you're concerned, Flower. And I'm beginning to see the appeal of having a wanted woman. You keep me on my toes. Honestly, I don't ever want to go back to normal and boring."

My face hurt from smiling so much. "You've finally come to the dark side. My plans are working."

I stood in the shadow of the greenhouse and watched my sisters and Kaitlyn cross the lawn. They were talking about the greenhouse. The pixies were happily telling them all about it while Noah brought Dani into his arms to kiss her passionately. It was so good to see my sister with a nice guy.

Dani's first husband was abusive and her second used her to fund his expensive hobbies. Noah would do neither and it was refreshing to know Dani was in the supportive relationship she'd always wanted. Going through two failed marriages could wreck a woman's confidence, yet Dani was strong enough to embrace life without backing down.

It would have been easier for her to shut down and not engage with Noah. It took courage to open up and give herself another chance. We'd had plenty of conversations and I was well aware of how much she'd learned from her mistakes. She'd given me the courage to open my heart and consider Lucas after he propositioned me.

"I can't believe how much we need for our magic," Kota commented as everyone joined us. "It's almost as much as we need for the business. Hey, do you think we can write off the supplies on our taxes?"

Kaitlyn chuckled and clapped Kota on the shoulder. "Because you will be holding the coven's celebrations here, you can absolutely write this stuff off as research or supplies. Are you guys ready? I have to get to a meeting in a bit."

The head witch was dressed like me, in jeans and a cotton t-shirt. The big difference between the two of us was her full rear end. Every time I saw her, I wondered if she had butt implants. No one's ass was that big and perfectly round.

Cami hung at the back of the group and hesitated when the others went inside the magical kitchen. I kissed Lucas's cheek, leaving him to approach her. "You're coming inside, right?"

Cami twisted the hem of her linen top in her hands. Cami preferred linen clothes to other fabrics. Likely because they were the closest to what she was used to when she was alive. "I don't want to intrude on the Twisted Sisters time."

I grabbed her hand. "Nonsense. You might not be a Twisted Sister, but you're part of this family. Everyone wants you to join us. I have a feeling we will be able to learn something from you."

Cami looked up with a smile and allowed me to lead her

inside. "I am pretty good at picking up on things. It didn't take you long to teach me how to read."

I loved seeing the uncertainty the former slave suffered from fall away from her. Owning your strengths was important. Some might call it boastful but I thought it provided the confidence needed in life, whether it was doing magic or running tours.

"That's right. Don't forget about the tour you walked us through. You convinced us you're ready to lead mundies through the plantation while telling them stories that will have them on the edge of their seats," I reminded her.

We'd agreed that she would take minimum wage for those hours, since we provided food and housing, plus keep all of the tips she was given during the tours. As a way to boost her confidence, I had her devise the plan for the entire experience. I wanted her to see that she could come up with the list of important things to show visitors throughout the property along with what to tell them.

"What do you guys want to start with today?" Kaitlyn asked as we entered the one room building. It cut off anything Cami might have said, but the former ghoul and slave took a seat at the end of the table without hesitation, so I stopped worrying about her and focused on the lesson we were going to learn.

Dakota lifted her hand. "I want to make a magical face cream that stops the signs of aging and reverses the fine lines and dark spots."

That sounded heavenly to me. If we could make our own face cream, it would save us a lot of money. "Yes, please!"

The others were just as excited about the idea. Kaitlyn pursed her lips. "That's actually a great idea. And you guys are in the best position to make this. We need bee venom and medical grade honey which basically means honey that has been sterilized by gamma radiation and provides an indicator of the level of the honey's antibacterial activity. In the mundane world that means it's registered for medical purposes and meets national requirements for medical product labelling. For us, we will use a spell to do the same thing."

Dani bounced off her stool and crossed to the shelves. "I brought jars of honey in here in case we would need it. We can sterilize this for our purposes, but how exactly will we get bee venom? It doesn't sound easy. We can't milk a bee's stinger. Can we?"

I winced when the image of me trying to hold a bee by its delicate wings while trying to push venom out its rear end. I'd be covered in more stings than the day Phoebe cast the spell that unlocked our magical heritage and broke the curse on Willowberry Plantation.

Kaitlyn lifted one eyebrow. "How do you think?"

Phi lifted a hand. "A spell?"

"You guys really are listening to me. Magic is the cornerstone of your world now. With time, thinking in terms of what spell, potion, or crystal can help will come to mind first," Kaitlyn reminded us that we did indeed still think like mundies.

She crossed to the window and opened it. "Talewen, can you bring some hyaluronic acid and collagen for the sisters to use?"

The pixies all flew to the window. "Are they making face cream first? That's an easy one to start with."

The head witch nodded. "It was Kota's idea and the perfect place to start." Kaitlyn moved back to the table and grabbed the honey, pouring some in each of our cauldrons. "Alright, we will sterilize this before moving on."

Dani used the wooden spoon Talewen had added to each spot and poked it into her honey. "Do we use *sterilitatem?*"

Kaitlyn shook her head from side to side. "We will use a

literal translation for this one to achieve what we want. *Sterilitatem a gamma radialis*. Picture heat cleansing the honey and bringing out the healing properties. When you create potions, the quality of your ingredients is of utmost importance which is why most witches grow their own herbs. They have control over any contaminants."

"Sounds like we got lucky with the pixies gift, then," I replied. I loved learning about magic. It gave me more skills to use in my life, whether I was facing off with Marie Leveau or getting ready for an event.

The seven of us went quiet as we followed Kaitlyn's directions, then cast the spell she'd provided. The familiar hum of my magic rose to the surface and powered the spell far easier than when we started practicing.

Dani's power was the closest to a dragon and fire engulfed her cauldron when she cast her spell. Kota fluttered her fingers and pink light flowed from them as she chanted her spell. Dea's was engulfed in bluish light, while Dre's was engulfed in the warmth of a hug. The air over Phi's felt frozen and Cami's had an earthy feel to it. It was astonishing how different each of them felt when we had all cast the same spell.

In the end, the smell of super-heated honey filled our magical kitchen. Phi paused after her honey was sterilized, to jot notes into a leather-bound journal with vellum pages that she had purchased for the creation of a family grimoire. I had engraved the Twisted Sisters symbol onto the cover, marking it as our own."Now for the hard part. Let's bespell the bees," Kaitlyn suggested. "Dani, can you grab an empty jar, please?"

We all headed out of the kitchen and walked across the lawn to the beehives. After sneaking a peek at Lucas, I refocused on the situation and the fact that I wanted to get Kaitlyn's opinion on my vision. I used the walk and told her what had happened, what I saw, and asked what she thought.

Kaitlyn tilted her head and met my gaze. "What did this mambo look like? Perhaps I can help you find her without having to go to Marie."

I recalled both visions. "She had black hair with blue streaks that matched the color of her eyes. I remember thinking of how striking the color was against her dark bronze skin tone. She also had on the ceremonial robes the mambos wore when they were here for the ritual. The only other thing I noticed was the skull tattooed on her left forearm. It had a top hat on that reminded me of the loa Samedi."

"I'm not familiar with this particular mambo but I'll ask around. Hopefully someone will have information for me. In the meantime, do *not* go to Marie. I know she denied the zombie attack. Assuming she's telling the truth, at a minimum she knows who did it. That doesn't happen without her." Kaitlyn turned to stare at Dea when she tried to say it was better to face Leveau now.

"She would not hesitate to punish the culprit. Her biggest mistake was assuming you six would be ignorant enough about her magic to call her on it. You can't trust her. When we have more information, we can develop a plan to pay the mambo or Marie a visit. The best approach will be to nullify her ritual space. Then we can ensure the sacrifice never happens. The loa's spirit needs a host soon or he will be sucked back to his realm," Kaitlyn finished.

This entire situation was way above our heads. It was dangerous and could end badly for most of us. However, we couldn't turn our backs. I was being given these visions for a reason.

Phi shielded her eyes with one hand while looking at Kaitlyn. "How much worse will we make things if we destroy this mambo's ritual space? We don't need to make any more enemies. We have children with no magical abilities."

Kaitlyn held up a finger. "Your kids have no powers, yet.

Whether or not they develop any remains to be seen. Anyway, we are not going to destroy the structure, only the symbols. The right cleansing spell will nullify the space entirely and make it useless for future spell work. A mambo willing to do this will repeat these behaviors at the earliest chance."

"Then we gather more information and look for this mambo before making any moves. This plan minimizes the chances of one of us being hurt," Dre said.

Kota, Phi and Dani agreed. I did too. I was about to open my mouth and ask how we could find the young woman to ensure she lived, but closed it. Kaitlyn's plan would prohibit the woman from being hurt. There would be no reason to hurt her if the space was nullified.

We'd reached the beehives. Kaitlyn pointed to the wooden top of the closest one. "Put the jar there. I'll cast the spell this time. Remember your intent is key to your enchantments. Here we want the bees to give us some of their venom, so I am going to picture them fluttering over the jar and ejecting venom from the glands in their stingers without needing to sting anyone or shed said stinger."

Kota pursed her lips while her forehead scrunched up. "You mean like they're picking up pollen with their faces, only this involves their backside and them giving something rather than gathering it."

Kaitlyn smiled and nodded. "Precisely. You'll want to step back and watch. There will be a flurry of activity shortly." The head witch focused on the hive for a few seconds before she chanted, *"Exe venenum."*

Kaitlyn's magic flowed from her and crackled in the air. It didn't sting like the feel of a vision. Instead, it was warm yet commanding. I could feel the pressure it exerted on the bees. The ease with which she managed to get thousands of bees to leave their home was astonishing. Within seconds the jar was obscured by tiny, buzzing, yellow and black bodies.

The noise of so many in action at once made my heart race as sweat coated my body. I flinched when Dani bumped into me. She'd closed the distance to stand next to me. When I looked over, I noticed she was breathing heavily, as well. I imagined it brought back the day that Phoebe did *the* spell.

After a minute or two, Kaitlyn chanted, "*Abscedo.*" The bees cleared and she lifted the vial that was now full of a cloudy liquid.

"Now we mix this with the honey and ingredients the pixies went to retrieve for us. After emulsification the cream will be ready. You can enchant the lotion to act faster or last longer, but I don't recommend it when you are dealing with magical bees like you have. I'll also leave some recipes for common potions so you guys can practice. These are the safest ones to start with."

Dani had a bounce in her step on the way back to the magical kitchen. "We can add this to the offerings in the souvenir shop. We have the drawing of the plantation so Lia can make the Christmas ornaments already. We might actually pull in a decent profit from the place with very little investment."

I was thinking the exact same thing. I felt better every day about leaving the security of my job and doing this full-time with Dani. I was happier than I ever had been. At times the burden of the visions weighed on me and made me ask myself why we couldn't pawn those situations off on someone else.

Then I recalled that I didn't hide from problems. I faced them head-on and that wasn't going to change now. Besides Lucas and Noah were the only ones to offer blanket support when we talked about what I'd seen. Kaitlyn offered her assistance but never offered to handle things outright. If we didn't solve them, no one would.

CHAPTER 9

DAHLIA

"Shit!" Kota called out as she added the aloe to the cauldron where she was practicing.

Instinct took over. I ducked and covered my head before checking to see what had happened. We'd cleaned up several messes in the past few hours. But we had several healing potions. One for indigestion, one for stomach aches, and another for congestion.

"Why the heck does aloe explode?" The calm now in Kota's voice told me we were no longer in danger.

Standing up straight, I glanced around and winced when I caught sight of Dakota standing on a step stool and reaching for the ceiling with a towel. "Maybe you should just wish that away. It looks sticky."

Kota scowled as she scrubbed even harder. "I'm not paying the cost of wishing for cleaning when I can save it for something worthwhile like the location of this freaking mambo."

I gasped and grabbed her leg, almost making her topple over. Dani jumped up and helped me stabilize her. "Sorry! But I hadn't thought of using your power before. Try wishing to discover who she is and see what happens. That would save a lot of trouble. And will let us know if we can use it in the future."

Dakota dropped the dirty towel and climbed down with a frown on her face. "I've never used it on a person before. It doesn't feel right."

I held up my hands and shook my head. "Then don't do it. We need to follow our gut when it comes to our powers. Kaitlyn and the others have theoretical knowledge of them, not real-life experience."

"Lia's right, Kota. It would be nice, but we don't want to put you at risk," Dani added.

Kota sat back down and shoved her cauldron aside. "What bothers me is the fact that my wish could lead to harm. I just wish there was a way to get around the guilt, so we could learn who she was and where she lived. Imagine what we could have avoided last time. You never would have been attacked, Lia."

Kota's eyes went wide as her hands flew to her mouth. "Oh, crap. What did I do?"

We all stared at each other for several silent seconds before Dre tilted her head to the side. "It seems it doesn't work on people after all. Your magic is instantaneous. Wish for some beignet fries."

My mouth watered thinking about the thin pieces of fried goodness. They were made from the same dough as normal sized beignets but were fried in bits the size of a French fry and covered in powdered sugar. They were the best and worst invention ever. You could eat ten times more than the regular ones because they were so little.

Kota rubbed her hands together. "I wish I had some beignet fries and lattes."

Over the past few months, I'd come to realize that unlike other spells, I couldn't always feel when we used our individual powers. The sweet smell of fried dough and roasted coffee beans told me Dakota's wish had been fulfilled. Behind her sat a large bowl of beignet fries and several white takeout cups with what I presumed were her lattes.

"I can't complain with those results," I said as I popped a fry in my mouth. The crispy fried goodness practically melted in my mouth. "It doesn't work on people. At least now we know."

Kota sipped a latte and made a sound of appreciation. "It would be nice if it were different. We just have to hope that Kaitlyn is successful in getting the mambo's name."

Dani groaned as she ate several of the treats. "We don't have many connections, but Nedasea and Brezok are asking around for us, as well. Brezok assured us that if the mambo has lived in New Orleans long, we will have her name by nightfall. Apparently, for as big as this city is, the magical population is relatively small."

The door opened and Dea walked inside. Her eyes lit up when she saw the latte and beignet fries on the table. "That smells delicious. I haven't had time to eat this morning. Mateo had his driving test, so I now have two licensed drivers in the house."

I remember the day my kids were able to start driving. It saved me from having to take them to early morning and evening swim practices. Although, I admit I actually missed taking Teagan after she got her license. I'd started the swim mom duties when Mackenna was six, and she was ten years older than Teagan, so I'd done it for almost twenty-five years.

"Enjoy it while you can. It's nice when you have minions to send on errands for you," I replied.

"It's the best when they start driving. Before you know it, they're going to be back to ask you to help with their kids," Dre added.

The ringing of Dani's phone interrupted our discussion. "Six Twisted Sisters, this is Dani. How can I help you?"

I had no idea who was on the other end of line. My heart started racing when Dani's eyes went wide. "Hold on. I'm going to put you on speaker phone so you can repeat that."

Dani pressed a button and set her phone next to the bowl of beignet fries. "Okay, Kaitlyn. Go ahead."

"Hello, ladies. I am calling to tell you I found the mambo and I am hoping you will join me at her house shortly." Kaitlyn sounded excited and more than a little nervous. By her own admission, she hadn't faced half of what we had in our short time as magical mutts.

Kota's eyes narrowed as she focused on the phone. "How did you find her? I thought it would take a lot more time."

Kaitlyn's sigh came through the phone. "I got lucky when I stopped to talk to a necromancer a half an hour ago. Now that they are no longer forced to report to Leveau, they're open to talking about what they know. When Temperance didn't recognize the tattoo, she suggested I go visit the guides running the voodoo tours. I had no idea Marie allowed her mambos to do something so audacious with mundies. I decided to approach some of the peddlers in Jackson Square, hoping one would recognize the description."

Jackson Square was a fenced in park in the middle of the French Quarter where public executions had taken place, as well as the location where Louisiana was officially made a part of the United States. For the past several decades people could get permits to set up tables and sell their artwork or offer their services. Surprisingly, there was a mixture of magical and mundane beings that sold stuff around the small park.

"I doubt it was your wish, Kota. They've never worked in a roundabout way like that," I reasoned.

"What do you mean?" Kaitlyn asked.

Dani explained the discussion we'd had a half an hour ago and the test we'd done to see if we could use Kota's magic to find people.

"It would be exceedingly rare if you were able to locate someone with a wish unless you were Tainted. Dealing with a person takes a great deal of Dark magic. We have natural protections in place that block magic like hers. I don't think I mentioned this, but we don't have love potions or spells that will make another fall for someone for the same reasons. Finding Lucinda was the result of good, old fashioned detective work," Kaitlyn explained.

Kaitlyn gave us an address and the five of us agreed to meet her there in an hour. My stomach refused to settle as we headed to the house to change into jeans and tennis shoes. None of us wanted to get into a fight with a powerful voodoo practitioner in shorts and flip flops.

I grabbed one of the machetes Kota had conjured a while back then headed to my car. I unlocked the doors and slid behind the wheel. "Is anyone else disturbed that this mambo only lives ten minutes away from Willowberry?"

Dre lifted the middle seat to allow Dea to get into the third row. "I can't help but wonder if she is the one that sent the zombies after us. I have no doubt Marie Leveau was behind this. However, I doubt she was the one to actually create them and give them their orders. Lucinda's location makes her a prime candidate."

Dani got in the seat behind mine. "Unless there are more mambos out here."

Kota scowled as she shut the passenger side door. "As disturbing as that is, we need to focus on how we are going to handle *this* mambo. We've got two machetes and unpredictable magic. I don't like our odds."

I winced as I realized she had a point. "Kaitlyn will be with us. We will follow her lead and cast what she does. Between the six of us, we should be able to manage something."

Dre stuck her head between the seats. "I looked up a spell to cleanse her space since that's our goal. Regardless of anything else, we need to have a clear picture of what we want to accomplish so in the heat of it we don't have to stop and think for long."

Dani clapped Dre on the back. "I was hoping to sit on the sidelines, sestra. However, being prepared is a much better option. We can't leave Kaitlyn to face this alone."

Kota nodded her head. "The only reason I'm in the car is because we've been underestimated at every step, and deemed weak, because we haven't been in this world long. That has given us the advantage in every situation. No one expects us to be more powerful together."

I chuckled and smiled at Kota. "Very true. I love the look on their faces when we beat them with a tenth of the skill." My heart raced the closer we got to the address.

"If we need more weapons, I'll wish for them. Next time though, I'm asking for kindjals. My girls told me they're smaller and easier to handle in hand-to-hand combat."

"How the hell do they know about kindjals? Annabelle is a teacher and Kora is a psychologist. Mia's a manager," Dani pointed out.

Dakota chuckled. "It's their obsession with some fantasy show on TV. One of the heroines carries two kindjals and fights with them."

The others discussed using weapons against a living person and whether or not they could actually hurt her as I drove. It was easier for me to remain focused on driving. If I thought too much about it, I would freeze up at the worst possible time.

I slowed to a crawl when I turned down Lucinda's street. There were more homes where she lived, but they were still spread out enough that we might be able to do this without a mundie seeing anything.

I parked behind Kaitlyn's car wishing I'd paid closer attention. We were right in front of the mambo's house. I preferred sneaking up so she wasn't prepared. We joined the head witch on the sidewalk, surprised she was alone. I expected to see at least one other witch with her.

"What's the plan?" Kota asked Kaitlyn.

Kaitlyn didn't respond. Instead, she was focused on the woman standing on the porch with her arms crossed. My breath caught in my throat. It was the mambo from both of my visions. This time she was dressed in a skirt and top rather than the ceremonial robe, but there was no mistaking the blue streaks in her hair. The color matched her eyes perfectly making me think it was a spell.

"What are you doing here?" Lucinda demanded.

Kaitlyn walked up the path that led to the door. "We're here to talk to you about the sacrifice you have planned to allow Baron Samedi to take on corporeal form."

The mambo's eyes widened fractionally before narrowing. "I have no idea what you're talking about. Now leave."

I shook my head. "We can't do that. We have a powerful seer that saw you killing an innocent woman."

The mambo laughed an evil sound that crawled up and down my spine like ants. She said something in Creole before she swirled her hands in a circle and pushed out at us.

I felt the heat and prickle of her magic as it headed toward us. I grabbed Kaitlyn and dove to the side while screaming, "Duck!"

I landed with the head witch on top of me. We rolled in

time to see the spell hit a large willow tree in the front yard. The bark blackened immediately as the leaves withered and went from vibrant and green to brittle and brown.

This wasn't going to end well unless we got a handle on things. Two more mambos raced across the lawn and joined Lucinda on the porch as she geared up for another attack.

I cast a protection spell around me then looked back at my sisters who were huddled together. I could see the shimmer around them. Dea was on the other side of the path staring at the three mambos. I didn't see anything around her body. Crap, I needed to get her to cast a bubble around herself.

I opened my mouth to tell her to protect herself when something caught my attention. A basement window was five feet from us. I could see the sacrificial table clear as day in the middle of the room.

"It's there," I told Kaitlyn.

She glanced over my shoulder then pulled a vial from her pocket. "Break that on the floor and chant, *purgo* while picturing the space being cleared out of all energy. Think of a bleach bath erasing every trace from the space. I'll distract them."

I nodded and rolled to the window to remain low to the ground while Kaitlyn jumped up and tossed a fireball at the mambos. Dre, Kota, and Dani joined the head witch in her attack of the mambos. Kicking the window in, I tossed the vial on the floor below. The glass shattered, sending bright green liquid all over the floor. I kept the image Kaitlyn described in my mind and chanted the spell.

The reaction was instantaneous. My magic came up against the voodoo spells and exploded. The smell of bleach and dead rodents wafted out the window along with black smoke. My eyes watered, making it impossible to see, while a coughing fit overcame me. I heard more glass breaking inside the house but didn't bother worrying about that. I needed to help my sisters.

Lucinda and her friends were pissed and throwing death magic wildly around the yard. I ran in a crouch and joined my sisters and Kaitlyn. I added my witch fire to the mix and sent amber flames to the porch.

The sound of a car door shutting behind us drew everyone's attention. The blood drained from my face when I saw who stepped out of the vehicle. Marie Leveau had arrived and from the look on her face she was angry.

Marie approached us while smoke continued to billow out of the basement window. "What the hell is going on here?"

A tall Asian man ran up the street and paused a few feet away. He was muscular but not too bulky. His suit looked like it belonged in a board room while his expression screamed that he was ready to take on a horde of demons. I had no idea who he was but Marie didn't look happy to see him which made me happy. "Fancy seeing you here, Marie."

Marie scowled at the guy. "What are you doing here, Xinar? This incident doesn't involve the Underworld."

Xinar chuckled while keeping his gaze locked on Marie. "UIS agents have an agreement with witches now. You know that. What's going on here?"

He must work for Aidoneus. He had told us he was the head of the Underworld Investigative Services, as well as the son of Hades. There was someone powerful looking out for us. I kept my fire at the ready while I told him about the vision that I'd had about Lucinda sacrificing an innocent woman for Baron Samedi to take possession of her body.

Lucinda flew down the stairs and headed right for me. It made me take several steps backward. "You made my ritual space unusable; you bitch! You're going to pay for that. You had no right. I haven't done anything."

Xinar stepped in between us and held up his hand. "Enough. You know well enough that sacrificial magic involving people is illegal." That didn't impact Lucinda who continued to move in my direction with her fists clenched at her sides.

Marie Leveau made a hand gesture, stopping Lucinda. "This woman isn't worth the effort. She's little more than a mundie. Her power of premonition is unreliable and incorrect." The Voodoo Queen shifted her piercing gray eyes in my direction. "You really should stop spreading lies. They tend to catch up to people in the worst possible ways. I'd hate to see you come to harm."

Xinar jerked his chin toward the sidewalk. "It's time to go now."

I looked at Kaitlyn who nodded in agreement. My sisters followed beside me as we went back to my car. We huddled together and watched Marie talking to Lucinda. It was all the confirmation I needed that the queen was involved in the plans for Samedi.

Xinar got my attention. Now that I really got a look at him, I had to admit he was an attractive man. His short black hair was neatly styled and his skin was so clear I doubted he had any pores. I preferred my rugged shifter to Xinar's pristine beauty.

"You have made some powerful enemies. I'd be careful if I were you," he said.

I smiled at him. "We've made some powerful allies in the process. I figure it balances out. But we will always follow our gut and do what's right. Besides, Marie Leveau hasn't liked us since we stopped her from stealing the bodies of some friends during a soul ritual. Stopping Lucinda from being able to finish what Marie started a few months ago is worth making her even madder. Samedi is an insane loa that doesn't have good intentions once he obtains a corporeal form."

Xinar laughed at the same time he shook his head. "I have a feeling the six of you will be trouble. Be careful. Marie Leveau is powerful and will simply regroup. I'm here searching for the skin walker and will keep my eyes and ears peeled for any news." We exchanged numbers with the UIS agent. "Now get out of here before they decide I'm no threat and resume attacking you guys."

We climbed into my car while Kaitlyn got into hers. Despite what Xinar said, I prayed that we'd dealt Laveau enough blows it would diminish her power and permanently stop her. Leveau's social power was already declining rapidly. I could only pray her acolytes and power were, as well.

CHAPTER 10

$\mathcal{L}$ ia grunted as she wiped the eyeliner from her lid and started reapplying it. This was the third time she'd done the same thing. "I'm not so sure this is a good idea, Dani. Why do they want us to meet their pack? It's worse than meeting the parents. He and Noah are important. What if they don't like us?"

I extended my hand for the pencil she was holding. "Give me that. I'm not sure why they're so insistent on us meeting everyone. We already met most of them at Lilly's wedding. We even have that anniversary party in a few weeks. And another mating ceremony this winter. I figure this gathering is a shifter thing. You know they aren't like mundies. It might be important, now that we are dating."

I drew a line close to her eyelashes, extending it past the corner then did the other eye. "There. How's that?"

Dahlia put her glasses back on and a smile broke out over

her face. "Perfect. Thanks. My vision sucks without my glasses. Sometimes even with my glasses."

I snorted. "Why do you think I won't let you behind the wheel at night? I'd be safer walking into a vampire den alone."

Lia smacked my shoulder then checked her outfit for the tenth time. "This shirt must have shrunk in the wash. It's tighter than it used to be."

After spraying my hair one last time, I wound my arm through hers and tugged her out of the bathroom where we'd been getting ready. "You look gorgeous. Lucas is already crazy about you. You have nothing to worry about."

Lia straightened her shoulders. "Thanks, sestra. I told myself I wouldn't do this with Lucas. I hate the insecurity and worrying about what he'll think of my stretch marks and extra pudge, but you know what? I'm not perfect and no amount of makeup or clothing will hide my flaws. I earned every scar and mark on my body. He needs to like me for who I am."

I was proud of my sister. It wasn't easy for most women to have pride in themselves when they reached middle age. The media had us believing we had to have flawless complexions and fit bodies with no marks whatsoever. The reality is that our bodies age and change, gathering the signs of the passing years.

I was in no better shape that Lia, I just wasn't as worried. Noah had already seen me naked. He hadn't flinched, either. In fact, he'd worshipped my body on more than one occasion, so I knew he liked what he saw. I prayed Lucas would be the same with Dahlia, otherwise I was going to have to have Noah kick his best friend's ass for me.

Speaking of the devils, as we reached the landing, we saw Lucas and Noah stood in our formal foyer talking with Cami. The look in Lucas's eyes told me I didn't have to worry about my sister. Shifting my focus, I nearly swallowed my tongue when I caught sight of the heat in Noah's gray gaze.

Turning the tables, I scanned my boyfriend from head to toe. A groan left me when I caught sight of the tight grey cotton stretched over his abs. He wasn't wearing a flannel tonight, but he had on the jeans that hugged his ass perfectly and the black boots that made him look a bit on the wild side.

His hair was longer than when I'd first met him and it was those tousled brown locks that did it for me. Noah grabbed me into a hug when we reached the bottom floor. His large hands were warm as he cupped my cheeks and pressed his lips to mine. He held me tight when I went to pull away. The closeness pressed every hard inch of him against me, making me want more. I gasped when he deepened the kiss, sliding his tongue in to tangle with mine. It took a herculean effort to make myself push against his chest and break the kiss. This was not the time and place to start making out. My cheeks were flaming by the time I parted from his hard body.

I cleared my throat and looked at Cami. "We will be back later tonight. You know where Dreya is if you need anything."

Cami smiled and shooed us out the door with her hands. "I'll be fine. Don't worry about me. Have fun."

Lia handed me my purse and walked out hand in hand with Lucas. Noah clasped my hand in his, as well. "We heard you guys had another run-in with Marie Leveau today."

I looked over at Lia as we walked to the parking lot and Lucas's truck. "Yeah. Kaitlyn found the mambo from Lia's vision and we neutralized her ritual space, making sure it couldn't be used to sacrifice anyone."

"We also met a UIS agent who is here searching for the skin walker," Lia added.

Noah opened the back door for me then went around and

joined me on the bench seat in the back. Lucas's expression was stormy when he pulled out of the lot. "What did this UIS agent want with you guys?"

Dahlia lifted a shoulder. "Nothing really. He warned us to be careful and said we'd made a powerful enemy."

I chuckled recalling her response to Xinar. "She also told the demigod we'd made powerful allies. It's nice to know we have someone in law enforcement on our side, as well. To completely change the subject, what is this pack gathering about?"

Noah gave me his reassuring smile while from the corner of my eye I noticed Lucas look over at Lia. "The pack started asking questions about us, so we wanted to clear things up for them. Worried wolves are dangerous. It's better that we lay it all out for them."

My stomach flipped, sending bile shooting up my throat like a geyser. What did that mean? It sounded serious. I'd been dead wrong to talk Lia out of panicking. This was going to blow up in our faces. Chances were high I was going to do something that would offend a shifter and make them challenge me.

I tugged my gloves higher up my wrist. I should have worn a long-sleeved shirt to make sure nothing came in contact with my skin. Noah's hand landed on my arm. I'd touched him so often that I didn't get visions from his clothing anymore.

"It's alright, Sunshine. There's nothing to worry about. It's all good," Noah promised.

Lucas sent Noah a look in the rearview mirror. The two of them exchanged a silent conversation before Lucas reached over for Dahlia's hand. "We wanted to wait and tell you but it'll do no good for you both to be worked into a frenzy by the time we arrive. I plan on telling the pack that I've found my Fated One."

Lia did an impression of a fish out of water when she opened and closed her mouth several times. I was confused for a split second by what he'd said. Then I realized he was saying Dahlia was his mate. The one woman meant for him.

Noah brushed a finger against my cheek. "I tried to tell you this when Lia was in the hospital but you didn't get it, so I'm going to say it plainly. You're my Fated One, Dani."

A squeak escaped my lips as it became my turn to play the fish. My mind raced a million miles an hour while my heart tried to keep up. I had no idea what to think or how I felt at the moment. I was stunned and terrified. Okay, so I knew a little about how I felt.

"What does that mean exactly? I just went through a divorce and moved into a phase in my life where I'm truly happy for the first time in decades. I have no desire to move out of Willowberry or make my sister leave."

Dahlia turned in her seat and I got a glimpse of how overwhelmed she was. "Yeah, what she said."

Lucas brought Lia's hand to his mouth and kissed the back of it. "I'm not asking you to change anything, Flower. I'm not even asking for a formal mating ceremony right now. I know you have your life and I'm proud of the woman you are and a big part of that is your relationship with your sisters. I would never dream of getting in the way of that."

My heart burst for Dahlia. Leo had been a good husband, but he had his quirks. He never helped with the housework and he got pissed when she spent time with us. He would tell her it was because she didn't discuss it with him but I knew better. He was jealous that we always laughed and had fun together.

From what I had seen, Lia had pulled away from Leo because of the way he talked to her at times. It was hard to want to get intimate or even just spend time with someone that snapped at you and told you the way you fed the kids or folded the laundry was wrong. These were additional reasons Dahlia was reluctant to get involved with someone again.

Lia watched Lucas so closely that for a second, I worried she was having a vision. She echoed some of what I had just been thinking. "That means a lot to me. I lived a life with someone that would berate me and say my sisters meant more to me than he or the kids did when I saw them a handful of times a year. But how do you know? I mean we've never even had sex, yet."

Lucas pulled her closer to him but she didn't move far because of the seatbelt. "It's difficult to explain. When I laid eyes on you my wolf howled in my head after claiming you as his. There's this sense of peace that settled over me knowing he was right."

"And a sense of completion that I'd never before experienced," Noah added making me look at him.

I tried to return Noah's smile but doubted I pulled it off. "Is that a wolf thing? I mean, I liked you right away and was drawn to you. Of course, I thought you were the sexiest guy alive; but nothing like you described."

"Yes, it's a shifter thing," Lucas replied. "We will have proof when we complete the mating because Noah's mark will appear on you and yours will cover his heart. I know this was a lot to take in and I can see you're both still absorbing it all. However, we're here. We will be letting the pack know what you are to us. Are you ready to do this?"

Dahlia looked at me and I shrugged. I had no idea what to think or do. "I have one question. Does this mean we *have* to stay together? What if we find we don't like each other?"

Noah's smile faltered and a grim expression replaced it. "I will never force you into something you don't want. Lucas wouldn't either."

There was more there, but I wasn't sure I wanted to hear

it right now. I needed to get through this party before my mind melted completely. Dahlia sucked in a breath and nodded. "Let's do this. But I am not saying anything. I barely remember my own name right now. I need time to digest it all."

Lucas parked the truck and leaned over to kiss my sister. I looked away and saw the longing in Noah's eyes. I couldn't make out with him while Dahlia and Lucas were practically jumping one another's bones in the front seat, so I turned to gaze out the window.

We were surrounded by trees with a neighborhood built around them. About a hundred feet in front of us I could see Noah's house with the others around his. Between Noah and his neighbor, I saw the orange flicker of a fire. Curious to see what pack lands looked like, I climbed out of the truck.

Noah was there wrapping an arm around my waist and leading me toward the houses. "As you likely remember, that's my house on the left and Lucas's on the right with the other pack members that live here spread out to both sides. Lucas and I are positioned to respond to any threats first."

Noah's house was reminiscent of a Creole cottage with a tiny porch covered in neatly potted plants. The blue shutters stood out against the white of the walls even in the darkness.

Lia and Lucas were next to us a second later and Noah was guiding me through the space to the center of pack lands. I had never been this far in before. The entire neighborhood had houses built in the Creole style with most being painted bright colors. There were sidewalks but no streets. And the sidewalks didn't extend to the center where the bonfire was raging.

At least a couple hundred shifters milled around a massive fire that was set in the middle of green space that was easily the size of a football field. They were talking, drinking and eating while music played in the background.

There were camping chairs brought out but there were no picnic benches. The space was covered in grass and had a handful of trees planted around, otherwise there was nothing else there.

Immediately, I understood why Lucas wanted to have Lilly's mating ceremony at Willowberry. We offered different spaces to have the celebration and the ceremony along with fountains, formal gardens and so much more.

Lucas held up a hand. "Shadowtail Pack!" Everyone outside went quiet, even the children. And all eyes shifted to their alpha. I moved next to Dahlia and grabbed her hand. We made quite the foursome with Lucas holding Lia's other hand and Noah holding mine.

I started shaking when Lucas announced that Dahlia was his mate. He told the pack that nothing was changing and there would be no ceremony for now. Noah went next and silence continued for several seconds. Lilly broke the shocked quiet when she lifted a bottle of beer and cheered her father. The rest of the gathering followed suit.

Before I knew it, shifters started coming up to congratulate Noah and Lucas before introducing themselves and welcoming us to the pack. I was hugged so many times my arms were getting heavy. I didn't work out and lifting my limbs that many times was taking a toll on me.

Noah must have felt how uncomfortable I was because he lifted his fingers to his mouth and whistled. "We can continue the welcome after I feed my mate. She's trembling from hunger and eyeing Nannette's gumbo."

I shook my head. I wasn't sure I could eat. Shifters had heightened senses and they likely smelled my fear. I needed to get over this before they looked down their nose at me. "It was the chicken fingers, not the gumbo. You know I'm a woman of simple tastes."

Noah laughed and tugged me to the food table where

there was everything from boiled shrimp to grits to etouffee and what looked like Cajun chicken with rice. I went right for the latter. It was one of my favorites.

Dahlia was next to me putting a taste of everything on her plate. She was far more adventurous than me. "Are they still staring at us?" She asked in a whisper.

I glanced around and was happy to see most had gone back to their conversations. "Some, but not all of them."

The scream of a child shattered the jovial, happy mood of the party. I dropped my plate and hurried to follow Lucas and Noah who were running to the other side of the bonfire.

I stopped short when I saw what was ahead of us. A zombie had a little girl by the throat. The flesh of the zombie's face was decayed in most places, leaving her skull showing through. Her dress was dirty and tattered while her eyes held that eerie hunger I'd seen when they attacked Willowberry.

"Get down," Lilly called out to Lia and me before she pulled us to the ground.

A wolf jumped over us and launched itself at several zombies heading through the space between houses. The wolf tore into the creature while I shifted wide eyes to Lia. "Marie is attacking us on pack land? That seems ballsy, even for her."

Some shifters gathered the children and took off running while others transformed into their wolf and attacked the dozens upon dozens of zombies now all over the place. Everywhere I looked I saw the reanimated dead. And they weren't attacking the wolves. They were trying to get to Dahlia and me.

I called my yellow witch fire to my hands just in time to set a dead guy, with maggots squirming in one of his eye sockets, on fire. He'd managed to sink his teeth into my arm before he went up in flames. I kicked him to the bonfire and left him to burn.

Next to me Dahlia was fighting against three zombies that had her arms stretched at her sides. Her amber flames dripped from her hands ineffectually. Lilly hadn't shifted into her animal yet. She was keeping the zombies from reaching me, so I helped Lia.

My veins felt like they had lava running through them as I was scratched and bit countless times. I chanted the spell for the magical bomb and was about to toss it when a zombie stumbled into me. Her stomach was missing so my hand went inside her body and that was where I ended up detonating the magical bomb. It promptly blew her to bits.

Dahlia grunted as she kicked one of the zombies in the nuts. "What did you do?"

"Magical bomb to the gut. Very effective." I repeated the process with the next zombie and didn't hesitate before moving on. Two of the dead exploded and the ones holding Lia's arms followed suit a second later.

We turned to face off with more enemies but were surrounded by wolves. The pack had formed a circle around us, to keep us as safe as possible. It was just in time, too. My legs threatened to give out from the zombie toxin and I caught myself on the back of the closest wolf.

I spotted Lucas and Noah tearing through the rest of the zombies about ten feet in front of us. The shifters spread out and started dragging the dead again bodies to their fire when no more surged into the central meeting place.

As the body parts piled up to our right, wolves started changing back so fast that within seconds there were dozens of naked people picking up the pieces and helping clean up while only a handful continued killing the remaining threat. I wrapped an arm around Lia and we leaned into each other so we stayed on our feet.

Pretty soon there was only one zombie left and it was flanked on each side by Lucas and Noah. Before the wolves could rip it to shreds, the zombie opened its mouth and spoke. "I told you that you would know when I was behind an attack. This is me coming after you."

Noah's jaws closed around the zombie's throat, cutting off whatever else Marie planned on saying to us. I shook so hard I toppled over, pulling Lia down with me. Between one frantic heartbeat and the next, Noah was there picking me up. Lucas grabbed Lia and they took us away from the carnage.

"Lucas, you bring your mate to my clinic, right now."

I scanned the area to see where the scratchy voice had come from. I spotted an older woman standing in a doorway waving her arms at Lucas and Noah. She looked like she suffered from osteoporosis and was bent practically in half. She had on a pink moomoo with green palm trees. The garment was obnoxious but not as bad as what she was wearing on her feet. No one should wear socks with Birkenstocks.

Noah pressed a kiss to the top of my head. "Wynona will treat your wounds and clear up any infections."

The pixies used a special concoction to keep any of us from suffering from flesh eating bacteria last time we fought zombies. "Does she make her own potions?" The question was out before I could sensor my thoughts.

Whether this healer bought them or made them didn't matter. I needed to ask what this attack meant for our standing with the pack, followed by what we needed to do about this blatant assault on Marie Leveau's part. Unfortunately, bile filled the back of my throat while my vision swam.

I blacked out for God knows how long because one second Noah was walking into a warm and cozy house and the next, I was whimpering as Wynona smeared paste all over my wounds.

"Stop whining. The pain will stop soon," Wynona snapped at me. "I have to treat this or your flesh will rot away and you will die."

Wynona's bedside manner left a lot to be desired. Lucas placed a hand on Wynona's shoulder. "These women didn't cower and let our people fight. They killed more than I did. They're true warriors."

Wynona grunted but her touch gentled. "You need to rest while this works and your body fights off the toxin. Both of you."

"Thank you. I know I'm not your responsibility." I didn't know what else to say to the woman.

Wynona started wrapping gauze around some of the deeper wounds. "Nonsense. You and your sister are mated to our Alpha and his Beta. There is no one more important than the two of you. I just hope you will be more careful in the future to not piss off someone like Marie Leveau."

"Should we have let the Voodoo Queen steal our friend's body? Because that's what we did to earn her ire," Lia snapped back.

"Enough," Lucas growled.

"No, Lucas. I want your pack to understand we aren't wandering around making false accusations. That's the rumor Marie is spreading when the truth is we helped thwart her plans to give Baron Samedi a body in this realm."

Wynona's surprise was as evident as her anger. Lucas explained about how the six of us were continuing to get in Marie's way and that tonight's attack was a direct result of our destroying a location she'd planned to sacrifice an innocent.

I half listened as Noah lifted me into his lap. My eyes were slipping closed as fatigue made it next to impossible to remain awake. I only wished my mind would shut off, as well. Instead, I was churning over what being Noah's Fated One and Marie's outright aggression meant for our lives and my ongoing relationship with Noah. I imagined he would have a hard time leaving my side after this.

CHAPTER 11

DAHLIA

I should have been exhausted like Dani, but I was oddly energized. The night had included too many truth bombs for my mind to shut off. "You can take me back to Willowberry. We will be safe behind the wards. We've added protections against the dead."

My heart raced as I considered the danger we'd brought to the pack. "I had no idea Marie would take such a huge risk by attacking us here. I'd have thought she would reconsider making an enemy of the pack."

Lucas grimaced and ran a hand over the back of his neck. "This was a message to the entire magical population in New Orleans as much as it was you and your sisters. We gave her our answer when we slaughtered her zombies. I've even asked some of my soldiers to deliver body parts to outside her lair in the cemetery. They're taking the one she used to give you her message. Marie is scrambling to regain the position of power she once held here. She's never been more dangerous than she is right now."

I swallowed the lump in my throat. "I'm so damn sorry. I never stopped to think of the ramifications to you and your people when I stood up to her. I knew I could stand with my sisters and we'd keep each other safe. I never meant for it to bleed over to your wolves."

Lucas turned on the sofa to face me. "There is nothing to apologize for. Someone has needed to unseat Marie for many centuries. Her ancestors have continued to carry on the tradition of the first Voodoo Queen and it has only gotten worse for the rest of us. The necromancers are forever grateful for your part in the events that freed them. The pack was taken off guard but they are backing me, and thus you and your family."

Guilt made my stomach sour and my head ache. "And they're doing that because I'm you're Fated One."

Lucas cupped my cheek and ran his thumb over my lower lip. "Yes. They will always protect my mate. Do you want to talk about that? I know it was a lot to drop on you. I wanted to wait until we got to know one another better but with your life in increasing danger, I needed you to understand why I will be sticking close to you as much as possible."

My heart swelled with love when I considered his words. The ramifications of what they meant weighed on me like a ten-ton elephant. I hadn't considered marrying anyone ever again and that's basically what being his mate was.

I leaned into his touch, allowing it to settle some of the nerves jumping around in my stomach. "I can't take any more right now. I don't even know what to think."

"I agree with what Dani said earlier, I can't move out of Willowberry. I can't explain it but that's where I am meant to be at the moment. It's like the six of us are tied to the land."

The smile Lucas gave me could light an entire room. "I don't mind. I'm not asking you to move in here with me. I'm not even asking that we perform the ceremony any time soon. But, at some point I will need to move in with you there or spend as many nights with you as you will allow."

My mind screeched to a halt. "You go from zero to sixty without pressing the brake."

Lucas's smile faltered and he pressed his lips in a tight line. "I want to be honest with you about everything. It's been hard to keep this from you. My wolf will drive me feral if I'm not at least close to you. I'm not saying it needs to be this month or the next six months. The more time I spend with you the longer my wolf will remain calm."

Kaitlyn had told us we needed to stop thinking like mundies. It wasn't exactly easy to do. Forcing the doubt, fear, and panic aside I considered things from his perspective. He was acting on how he felt and what he needed. There was nothing wrong with that.

"Alright, that's fair. I can tell you I am not ready for you to move in with me. Not even close. But a few nights here and there, doesn't sound so bad."

Lucas pressed his lips to mine. I felt the passion banked in his kiss. Anticipation curled my toes, so I was disappointed when he pulled away. "I'll take whatever you'll give me, Flower. I do have one hard limit. I don't want you going out alone to face unknown situations and paranormals without me. My primal side has to protect you. I can't be away from the pack all the time, but splitting my time will work. Not to mention it'll give others in the pack the chance to grow and take on more responsibilities."

Buying the plantation had been the next phase in our lives. A new journey I was taking with my sisters. That had turned into something far bigger than any of us could have dreamed up. I'd gone from a social worker for Child Protective Services to a party planner to a witch and magical detective.

One thing was certain, life wasn't boring. And the thought of having this sexy shifter as mine for the rest of my life sounded pretty darn good to me. *What if you're not sexually compatible? Do you really want to go back to living a celibate life?* The answer to that was a resounding no.

My desire for Lucas was always burning in the background. Now that I thought about him, it went from a simmer to a roaring boil. It was up to me to make a move. He was taking things slow like I'd asked which I appreciated.

I wasn't particularly eloquent or sexy in that graceful way and I almost talked myself out of moving forward. I don't need to change who I am to be loved. The mantra was one I'd been telling myself since I got my magic and it gave me courage.

"We have plenty of time to figure out the details. Right now, we need to focus on you and me and making sure we are compatible." A shudder worked its way through me as I shifted positions and straddled his lap.

Lucas's eyes went wide at the same time his hands landed on my hips and held me in place. "I like how you think, Flower."

I was shivering by the time his lips descended on mine. His hands moved under my top and unclasped my bra. His touch was like a brand, burning me everywhere he placed his fingers.

He kissed me until I was breathless. When he broke away, he tugged my shirt over my head and tossed it aside. The way he scanned my torso erased any insecurities that remained. There wasn't even the smallest hint of disgust in his eyes.

Suddenly wanting to be naked with him, I lifted my hips

and unbuttoned my jeans. My mouth went dry when he set me on my feet and divested me of my pants and underwear in a move so fast my head was spinning.

I reached for his shirt. He helped me by pulling the soft gray fabric over his head and added it to the pile. When he leaned back against the sofa, his gaze landed on the thatch of curls between my thighs. Pleasure stole through me making my core tingle. His eyes felt like they were caressing the bundle of nerves at the juncture of my thighs. The hunger there was beyond anything I'd ever experienced.

Don't get me wrong. I'd had sex plenty of times. It was just that none of my previous partners including Leo, had ever looked at me like Lucas did. I jumped when his hand brushed my inner thigh. As good as it felt to have him look at me like that, it was even better when he touched me.

"Are you alright? We can stop if you want." He pulled my leg to the side without waiting for me to respond.

"Never been better," I croaked. Anticipation was once again putting me on edge and heightening the entire encounter.

"That's good to hear because I have plans for you and that building ache." Lucas cupped my sex and pressed a kiss to the underside of one breast.

I gasped and remained as still as possible. I didn't want him to stop. The wonderful man that he was, he didn't make me wait long. A groan left me when his fingers slid through my soft folds. It wasn't all that surprising that they were instantly coated in my arousal.

Holy crap on a cracker. I'd never gone from turned on to coiled and ready to explode so fast. My body responded to his every touch like I was a canvas he was painting, soaking up every stroke and caress.

Lucas shifted closer and pressed his lips to mine. This

time, I took over the kiss. My tongue pressed against his mouth and forced its way inside. My arousal filled the air as I wriggled against his hand. I should have been embarrassed by my behavior but I was too busy giving myself over to the pleasure of the moment.

Our tongues resumed the sensual dance with a fast and urgent tempo that heightened my need for him. Every cell in my body demanded more. There was still a barrier stopping me from taking what I needed.

"You still have your pants on," I complained against his mouth.

Lucas trailed kisses from my mouth to my jaw and lower. "I need to get you ready for me before these come off. I'm bigger than the average man and you said it had been a while for you. The last thing I want is to cause you pain."

"I don't believe it's been long for you at all. You're too sexy for women to stay away from." The words flew from my mouth as my hands roamed over his chest. I hadn't meant to say what was running through my mind. I truly couldn't comprehend how a man this attractive hadn't been with a woman for a week let alone a month.

Lucas surged to his feet and wrapped his arms around me. "I never said I hadn't been propositioned. I just wasn't interested."

A smile spread over my face. Lucas made me feel like the only woman in the world and it wasn't just what he said. "You sure know how to make a girl swoon."

I groaned and looked down when I felt something hard pressed against my stomach. There was a significant bulge in his jeans. Lucas fused his lips to mine, successfully distracting me.

One hand went between my legs while the other trailed up my torso to latch onto a breast. The way he tweaked and pulled at my nipple, made me mewl against his mouth. My back arched and my body shuddered as his touch gave me more pleasure than I'd had in years.

Breaking away from my lips, Lucas dipped his head to pay homage to my nipples. I screamed when he closed his mouth around one rigid tip and sucked hard. I couldn't help it when I grabbed his head and held him to my breast while his hand continued to stroke the bundle of nerves between my legs. I writhed and moaned, seeking release from the building tension.

Lucas pulled back and sucked in a breath before he ran a hand up one of my legs. He used his finger to spread the glistening folds between my limbs. He licked his lips making me think naughty thoughts. I suddenly wished I knew what he was thinking when he looked at me.

Did he like the curves of my hips? Or the way my body quivered unabashedly from his touch? What about the stretch marks from carrying my three babies?

His hand found purpose between my thighs, and his fingers delved deeper. A growl escaped my throat when he touched a nerve deep inside that nearly triggered my climax. I lifted one leg and rubbed my core against his hand. The way Lucas stared at me told me he loved everything he saw.

"Holy shit that feels incredible," I whispered.

I practically detonated when Lucas removed his finger from my body and licked it. His eyes slid closed as he tasted my desire. It was salacious and debauched and everything I wanted.

His gray eyes stayed glued to my whiskey ones when his touch returned to my clit. A moan slipped past my lips, and my hips surged toward him. It was beyond my control. It had been entirely too long for me and my body was relishing the pleasure he gave me.

Lucas's eyes darkened as he leaned back in and nipped my

lips. "You're absolutely perfect. To watch you come alive is a sight to behold."

I opened my mouth to debate his statement, but my mind went blank the second he flicked my sensitive bundle of nerves. There was no room for anything but us coming together.

Lucas was thorough in his approach to getting me ready. His palm rubbed my clit while his fingers thrust in and out of my core. His mouth went back to my breast, and he licked and sucked and nipped my turgid flesh.

My legs gave out making Lucas catch me before I fell in a heap. He laid me on the sofa then went back to teasing my body. A second later he pinched my clit. My core tightened around the finger he had inside my sheath and my eyes rolled back in my head. Mini orgasms spread through me at the same time my thigh muscles clenched along with my core. The coil in my body was ready to explode in a big way.

"More, Lucas," I moaned. He added a second finger and catapulted me over the edge as a big climax had me quivering from head to toe.

"Ahh!" My scream left me as his fingers moved in and out of me, and I rode the waves of bliss.

As the spasms subsided, Lucas withdrew his fingers then draped his large frame over my body. His bare chest pressed into my aching nipples, but it was the hard length against my hip that grabbed my attention.

"You're naked," I observed as I panted unable to catch my breath.

I was so lost to my own pleasure that I'd missed him taking off his pants. That had never happened to me before and I didn't understand why it did with him. I felt bad about being so selfish and not giving him anything in return.

He chuckled against my neck where he was kissing and

nipping my flesh. "You're so damn sexy when you come apart that I couldn't wait to get inside you, Flower."

His shaft pulsed against my leg making me ache for more. My hand went between our bodies, and I wrapped my fingers around his cock. A tiny gasp escaped when I felt how thick he was. He wasn't kidding when he said he was bigger than most guys.

I stroked the hard flesh loving how silky smooth it felt while also being hard as stone. I squeezed tightly before moving my fist up and down his long length. It was my turn to enjoy Lucas's groan. He was even sexier with his mouth parted and his eyes on fire with desire for me.

"Gods your touch is nothing short of exquisite" His voice was low and husky, arousing me all over again.

I looked at what I could see of him, taking in every detail. One day soon, I would make him pose for me so I could get a good, long look. My finger ran over the spongey tip of his cock and moisture leaked onto my skin. The feel of him distracted me for several seconds.

Lucas bent and placed a tender kiss to my lips. Nothing inflamed me like my wolf. He shifted and his shaft popped out of my hand to rub against my core. I was going to combust again. It was so easy for him to get my engine revving. It was like he had a direct link to my pleasure center.

"I need to be inside you." Lucas's breath puffed against my mouth adding to the erotic moment.

"Are you sure you'll fit? It reminds me of a summer sausage." I snuck another look. It had grown bigger in the past few minutes.

Another sexy chuckle left his throat. "Summer sausage, huh? Don't worry. I'll fit perfectly. I'll go slow and easy, I promise. Just relax and enjoy it."

Leaning on one elbow, Lucas slid the blunt tip through my aching folds, hitting my sensitive clit. My insides melted, and the coil tightened in my abdomen again. Suddenly all that mattered was having another orgasm.

Lucas's mouth returned to mine. His lips teased mine while his tongue darted into my mouth. Just as I was getting caught up in his kiss, he pushed his swollen head into my tight sheath a fraction of an inch.

I cried out as he stretched me to the point of pain. Part of it was his size, and part was the fact that I hadn't been with a guy for years. The pressure from his invasion burned for several seconds until his hand brushed down my side.

"You feel amazing, Flower. I'm not sure how long I can hold back." There was a hint of embarrassment in Lucas's voice.

I cupped his cheek and nipped his lower lip. "Good thing you have the stamina of a wolf, then."

Lucas threw his head back and laughed at that. I sucked in a breath because it caused his shaft to pulse and throb inside while moving enough to spread my arousal around and ease the way.

"For once rumor is going to serve me well. I promise this isn't going to be the end tonight," he replied.

His promise was followed by his mouth traveling to my breast. He licked a nipple and the sensation sent a wave of pleasure through my body that loosened my core. Lucas snuck his hand between our bodies and rubbed my sensitive bundle of nerves.

As he strummed my clit, my hips automatically responded and within seconds, I was moving. He slid out then back inside deeper than before. His passage was easier that time making me realize the nerves inside my vagina had never been stimulated like this. The sound I made then sounded more feral than anything.

"You good?"

"Never felt like this. So good," I managed to reply. It wasn't eloquent but it was honest and all I could manage.

He pulled out and surged back in, pushing further. I spread my legs wider, allowing him more access. His thumb pressed on my clit, and his mouth nibbled my neck. His thrusts were a mix of hard and soft.

I wrapped my arms around his neck and focused on how good he felt. Lucas was gentle as he moved his hips, pushing in and out of me with a steady rhythm. "More?"

I nodded my head. "Hell yes."

Gradually increasing the tempo, he gazed in my eyes, connecting with me in the moment. It made it even more intimate than it already was. His shaft was an iron rod pistoning in and out of my center. Between his gaze and his cock, my desire took control and the coil in my core tightened once again.

Lucas twined his fingers with mine and brought them over my head. His thrusts intensified, and I gave myself to him completely in that moment. He groaned against my flesh a second before he bit into the curve where my shoulder met my neck.

The sharp burn of his teeth as he marked me sent me over the edge, and my climax barreled through me. His momentum picked up before he thrust deep inside and grunted. His head went back, and he howled as his seed spurted in an explosive rush.

I felt every jerk in my core as he filled my womb. My orgasm continued as we came together as one. It was the greatest high of my life, and I never wanted it to end. Reality would be harsh, so I enjoyed the way Lucas felt inside me.

Lucas pressed his forehead to mine. "That was incredible. Let's move this to the bedroom so I can make love to you properly this time."

I groaned when he pulled out then laughed when he

picked me up and tossed me over his shoulder and carried me down the hall to the bedroom. His hand landed on my ass making my skin tingle.

There were so many reasons we should stop and prepare for what Leveau might send our way next, but I wasn't letting that ruin what was shaping up to be the best night of sex in my life. We both needed this more than we needed a plan.

CHAPTER 12

DANIELLE

"I feel like I'm doing the walk of shame," Lia muttered as we walked to the backdoor of Willowberry. We never used the front door because this entrance was closer to where we parked.

I waved to Noah as Lucas turned onto the street and out of sight then nudged Dahlia's shoulder. "You aren't some notch on Lucas's belt, Lia. You're his Fated One."

Lia groaned and ran a hand over her face. "That's like forever, Dani. No divorce. I'm not sure how I feel about that."

I opened the door and held it for Dahlia to go inside the house. My heart lurched when she said that. I'd been divorced twice. Not that I'd planned either, or wanted another. It was the idea of not having a way out if I needed one.

"Did Lucas tell you what that meant for you?" I winced when I saw Dre and Kota in the kitchen cooking. I wasn't sure I was ready for them to know about what Lucas and Noah had said about us being their Fated Ones.

Dre looked up from cleaning okra. "Did Lucas tell Lia what?"

Dahlia glared at me then grabbed an energy drink and a tall boy from the fridge. She handed me the latter. "A lot happened last night. Lucas and Noah wanted us to go to this party on pack land so they could tell us and their shifters we are their Fated Ones. In the middle of celebrating, Marie Leveau had zombies attack us. She even spoke through one of her reanimated dead telling us it was her behind the assault."

Dakota dropped the wooden spoon into the large pot on the stove as she turned to face us. Her jaw hung loose and her eyes bugged out like a pug's. "I don't even know where to start with all of that."

Cami walked into the room then with a frown on her face. "Good morning. Is everything alright?" She looked around at everyone. "I worried when you didn't come home last night. Did something happen?"

Dre snorted. "You could say that. Lia and Dani mated their shifters and Marie Leveau sent zombies after them and the pack."

I lifted a hand when Cami started shaking worse than dried beans in a pair of maracas. "First of all, they told us we were their Fated Ones. We did *not* get mated last night. But the rest is true."

Kota fished the spoon out and rinsed it off. "We need to deal with this one thing at a time. The fun stuff comes first. What, precisely, does being a Fated One to a shifter mean?"

I had been out of it the night before, so Noah and I hadn't talked much more after we got out of the truck earlier in the evening. "It means that I was made for Noah. Or so he says.

Apparently, shifters only get one Fated One in their lives. It's pretty rare to find your other half."

Lia took a drink then set her can down and grabbed our Twisted Sisters reusable water bottles. "Lucas said if I don't want to be with him that he will never be with another woman. I'm it for him. He also told me that he isn't asking me to get mated any time soon, but that he will need to spend more time with me. He talked about moving in with me, or even just spending a few nights a week together."

Sweat dripped down my spine when I considered Noah telling me the same thing. I'd had two bad marriages and was not keen on jumping into something that serious right now. Not to mention that my energy and focus was on making the Six Twisted Sisters event planning company a success. Willowberry and the cases we kept finding ourselves embroiled in took up most of my time.

Dre went back to prepping the okra. "This house is big enough to accommodate the five of you and, eventually, we will have the other buildings done if anyone wanted to move out of here. Although this place can't sit empty day and night."

I held up my hand. "I am not moving out of Willowberry. I love it here. I can't imagine a better set up for me. I have no desire to live on pack lands. This is where I'm meant to be. But that's getting ahead of ourselves."

Lia scooped ice from our nugget ice machine into our water bottles then handed me mine. "We have to think about a compromise to propose to the guys. Lucas made it clear that if we keep them at a distance their wolves can go feral. I spent some of last night thinking about a plan and was thinking we could move into the rooms that are done on the lower floors but only sleep there when we have the guys over. I don't know about you, but I'd rather stay close to each other when we're here alone. That is if it's alright with you guys and Cami."

Cami looked like a deer in headlight. "Why would you ask me? I don't own this place. You guys do."

I paused in pouring Pepsi into my bottle to look at the woman who had died a slave hundreds of years ago only to be resurrected as a ghoul. "You live here, so you should have a say. We would never force you to live with someone that made you uncomfortable. Worst case scenario, if you don't like it, we move up fixing one of the houses because I like Lia's idea. It keeps things the same most nights while giving the guys some peace of mind."

Cami sniffed and wiped the tear that fell down one cheek. "No one has ever cared what I thought. I'd never deny your mates. I feel safe with Lucas and Noah. They always help keep us safe."

Kota shook the spoon in the air. "After Marie openly attacked you guys it'll probably be good to have them here. Steve can't defend you all from the paranormals that come our way and we're not exactly warrior princesses."

Lia fluffed her hair. "Speak for yourself. We will have to make sure Phi and Dea are okay with the arrangement."

Dre rolled her eyes. "As if they'd tell you no. It'll be nice to have them here more. We have all this land and more projects than we can shake a stick at and having them here will make the work go faster. Maybe they'll even bring some of their shifters with them from time to time."

"You better be careful. Lucas is their alpha, you might find them setting up a secondary site here," Cami warned with a chuckle.

The idea wasn't abhorrent after what we'd experienced last night. Yes, we had wards here, but we could only make them so tight because we were a venue that hosted events for all sorts of people. The only direction anyone could approach us was from the parking lot. The protections there allowed others to enter our property.

"You might be onto something there. Fighting the zombies was relatively easy last night thanks to the shifters." Not that I had come away unscathed, but I hadn't feared for my life like when they had ambushed us here at Willowberry. "It would be nice to have some of them live on the property for a while. Marie Leveau is seriously pissed off at us and I'm afraid of what she will do next."

"I guarantee several will come here for us," Lia said. "You saw how they surrounded us and tried to keep the zombies away."

"You must not have heard Wynona last night. She didn't like that we brought danger to her people," I replied.

Lia winced. "She wasn't happy at first. After you passed out, she was worried sick. I swear she took your blood pressure five times making sure you weren't getting worse."

"We can ask about that later," Dre said as she pulled out her phone. "If Lucas and Noah are going to be part of this family, it's time they meet some of the others."

My hands flew out to grab her phone. "What? Why? It's too soon."

Kota pursed her lips. "You're going to invite them to stay a few nights a week. That means everyone will meet them eventually. There's no time like the present."

Dre lifted the paring knife she was using. "We've already started a big batch of shrimp creole. We can add more sides and be all set. You invite Noah, Dani. And you make sure Lucas will be here, Lia. I've texted the fam."

Looked like family dinner was happening. I grabbed my phone and sent Noah a text message. I knew better than to try and stop the train. It was how we worked and was one of the things Leo used to give Lia a hard time about. She missed out on so much because he didn't want her there. Knowing the moments that Dahlia lost with our mom taught me these weren't times I wanted to miss.

The look Lia shot me told me how uncertain she was about asking Lucas. I squeezed her hand. "He needs to learn now what matters to you. He can choose not to be a part of it, but that doesn't mean you have to miss out, as well."

I regretted not telling her that earlier in her life when I noticed Leo pulling that stunt. No one deserved to be punished for wanting to spend time with their family. Or berated to get them to back down and give up something precious to them. I would never speak ill of Leo to Dahlia, but I wouldn't let her make the same mistakes, either.

I smiled when she typed her message and hit send. We both got responses at the same time. I looked up at Kota. "How many pounds of shrimp are you cooking? We've got two shifters coming to dinner for sure."

"We could always pick up a couple racks of ribs to go with it," Cami suggested. "Shifters like meat."

Dre waved the suggestion away. "Steve picked up twenty pounds of shrimp when he went to Bayou La Batre the other day. We can defrost them easily. You'd better make more base, Kota."

Lia grabbed the celery and green peppers from the fridge, handing them to Dre to chop, while Cami went to the pantry and got more chicken stock and tomatoes. I loved how my family came together in a pinch. It was one reason I couldn't imagine living away from them. Having Dre and Steve close and Lia in the house made me happy. I preferred to live with, or at least close to, my village.

* * *

I BROUGHT the bowls and silverware outside, unsure why I was so antsy. I wasn't a young woman about to approach her boyfriend and propose that they quasi-move in together. I was a middle-aged divorcee with three grown kids and a business of my own.

"Kota's grabbing the garlic bread from the oven now. I hope your boyfriends don't take too long, I'm hungry and this creole looks delicious," Steve remarked as he carried the big pot of food my sisters had been making when we arrived home earlier.

It wasn't my favorite dish but not much was. Thinking about how picky I was made me doubt my maturity. I had the palate of a six-year-old with my favorites being fried chicken, bean and cheese burritos, and Dea's chicken tortilla soup.

Of course, that was a simplistic list and did not include everything I liked. However, I wasn't adventurous with my food choices.

I scanned the parking lot and chewed on the corner of my lip. I'd known Steve since I was a young girl. He used to tease me, although he never made me cry like he had Lia on more than one occasion.

"They will be here soon. We can start eating before they get here, though." That sounded better to me because Steve and Jeff would go back to watch the game at Steve and Dre's house while we talked to Noah and Lucas.

Lia grabbed my arm and pulled me aside when Maliko, Jeff, and Tucker walked out the backdoor carrying side dishes. There were fried green tomatoes, salad, fried okra, and hush puppies.

Dea's boys were running around the lawn to our left playing with Justin, Phi's son. Phi's daughter, Rachel, was finishing up some homework somewhere in the house. My kids were all grown and out of the house, either at college or on their own. It was the same with Dre, Kota and Dani.

Lia grabbed my biceps and shook me once. "We aren't

going to talk about staying here during dinner. I don't want Steve giving me shit. I might throat punch him if he tries to make a fool of me. Or maybe I'll hex him to have erectile dysfunction."

I laughed as I extricated my flesh from her grip. I understood her concern. Steve seemed to enjoy picking on her. Likely because she made it so easy for him. "I agree whole heartedly. None of the others need to be involved. I'll talk to Noah later and you can tell Lucas when you're alone. For now, we'll eat and let them get to know everyone. Speaking of, we'd better go rescue them from the inquisition."

Tucker, Jeff, and Steve had surrounded Noah and Lucas the second they stepped out of Lucas's truck. Lia and I hurried over to join the group right as Steve asked about an electrician. Steve usually did the work himself but, given the addition he was building onto their house, he had enough on his plate.

I hugged Noah, pulling him to me. "How was the rest of your day?"

Noah placed a quick kiss to my lips. "It was long, but we're almost done with the renovations on our current project."

"That's good. How are things after last night's attack?" I meant to keep the conversation to light topics but, based on the way all of my sisters' husbands looked our way, I wasn't off to a good start.

"There haven't been any more signs of zombies," Noah replied with a shrug.

Tucker grabbed a bottle of beer and popped the top then held it out to Noah. "Should those of us that don't live behind wards be worried?"

Noah took a sip of his beer and shook his head. "Not at all. Marie isn't aware the six sisters don't all live together. And we will keep it that way."

"Not to mention I have pack members patrolling your neighborhoods looking for anything suspicious," Lucas added. "It wouldn't hurt to have Kaitlyn help cast protections around your houses, as well."

Kota and Dre walked out with baskets smelling of garlic heaven. "Time to eat," Kota called out. The boys came running and Rachel came hurrying out of the house.

"Thanks, man," Tucker told Lucas as he took a seat next to Phi.

Noah's eyes widened as he took in the covered area where the carriages used to pull up. It was situated between the main house and the exterior kitchen. I laughed and patted his chest. "It's a lot, I know. And this isn't even half of my immediate family. Most of our kids aren't here and none of my brothers or their families were able to make it tonight."

Noah sat next to Lucas at one of the tables and I took the seat next to him. A smile crossed Noah's face as he watched everyone grab some food. "Your immediate family is as big as the pack."

I snorted. "There were ten times this many people there last night. It's the noise and laughter that makes it seem like there are just as many."

The dinner was far better than the night before. We ate and talked until it was time for Phi and Dea to put their kids to bed. After saying goodbye to the others, I picked up a pile of dirty plates and carried them inside the kitchen. Noah gathered more and followed behind me.

My heart was hammering in my chest now that it was time to talk about them staying here. "We talked about the Fated One situation today and we have a proposal."

One of Noah's eyebrows disappeared beneath the fall of dark brown hair on his forehead. "That sounds ominous. I'm almost afraid to hear it after you describe being my other half as a *situation*."

I placed the dishes next to the sink and turned on the water as I tried to think of a way out of the mess I'd already made. "I'm nervous. I want so many things in life and you are one of them, but I cannot give up my dream for a guy again. I've wasted too much of my life and worked too hard to get here. I'm falling hard and fast for you and that scares me enough. I know how important what you want, and need are, as well, so I am hoping that you will be willing to stay here with me a few days a week."

Lia turned off the faucet I'd left running. "I guess we're doing this here and now. Right now, we live on the third floor which will remain private when we start tours. However, the walls are thin and the rooms aren't that big. Dani and I will move into rooms on the second floor, so there is plenty of space if you want to stay with us here."

Cami set the platters on the table, ducked her head and hurried from the room. Lucas scooped leftover creole into a glass container and smiled. "It sounds perfect. It gives me time with the pack and you, too."

"We can work on any projects you have while we are here," Noah offered.

Lia laughed at that. "Dani will keep you so busy you'll go home just to get a break."

I dumped soap in the water and started washing the dishes. "True story. Will you rinse?" I asked Noah. He pecked my lips and took the plate I was holding out.

"I was thinking," I began while I continued scrubbing some silverware. "With the dangers Marie poses right now, perhaps some of the pack might want to stay here at the plantation, too. We can work on renovating buildings where they can stay. I'd feel safer if we have more protections in place. We can't have impenetrable wards as you know and that leaves a weakness that can be exploited. I know it's asking a lot and I understand if it isn't possible."

Noah's hand lingered on mine when he went to take a bowl from me. "Lucas and I have discussed that very idea. We were going to suggest it but weren't sure how you would take it. Knowing there are others here, when we aren't, will ease our wolves a great deal."

Lia smirked at me. "Told ya."

I rolled my eyes. "Excuse me for doubting others would be willing to sacrifice for us to have our happiness."

"I know what you mean. It feels selfish even asking it," Lia added.

Lucas scowled at Dahlia. "You are the least selfish women I've ever known. You're allowed to have your happiness and ask for what you want. How else will you ever get it? Besides, I would move the entire pack here if that's what it took."

"I'd happily move to Willowberry," Noah said.

I pointed a fork at him. "Because I'm your Fated One. Not everyone will feel that way. Don't make anyone come here on our account. Only those that want to be here."

Noah stepped closer to me so his side brushed along mine. "I would do it for my alpha. And to keep the Twisted Sisters safe. Lucas and I are not the only ones that see how important you and your business are to the magical world."

"You guys provide a place where we can celebrate and be ourselves without fear of being seen by mundies. There aren't many places we can do that. And then there is the way you're shaking shit up," Lucas added. "Word has already spread that you survived yet another of Marie Leveau's attacks. You've given hope to those that never dared to dream about being out from under her thumb."

Dahlia gaped at Lucas. "Like who? I thought she had her mambos and the necromancers and they're already free."

Lucas and Noah shared a look before Noah sighed. "The vampires for one. Marie claims the banshees, as well. There are also the demons, nightshades, ghosts, specters and phantoms."

I couldn't fathom how this woman had the time or desire to deal with all these creatures. "I'm guessing it's not possible to kill her, so how do we handle this situation? We can't back down now."

Noah took the plate from me and dropped it into the sink then brought me into his arms. "We take it one day at a time until a solution presents itself. She isn't immortal, so she can die, but with the loa backing her it is incredibly dangerous and difficult. But I will be here for you no matter what. Knowing the pack is on your side will make her think twice. It might even make her stop. For now, at least."

I looked up at him and saw nothing but adoration shining back at me. I refused to label it love. It was far too early for that. "But why would you risk your people for my sisters and me?"

Noah cupped my cheeks and that look intensified. "I would do anything for you, Sunshine. I would overhaul my entire life if that's what it took."

I buried my face in his chest. My emotions were on over-load for the second night in a row. What was worse was how my mind kept whispering that Noah couldn't possibly be that willing to make sacrifices for me. In my experience men lied and manipulated to get what they wanted.

Some were cruel and cut a woman down in the process while others said the right things and seemed supportive while using her without making it obvious. In the end both types of guys didn't give a shit about the woman.

Stop it. Noah is not like those guys. He cares for me and would never hurt me. I would remind myself of that fact as many times as it took for it to stick. I refused to hurt him because I married assholes in the past. They'd taken enough from me. They weren't getting between me and Noah, as well.

CHAPTER 13

DAHLIA

"We've got another one!" I shouted, then laughed, as I hung up my phone. I loved movies from the eighties and *Ghostbusters* had been a favorite. Of course, it was all the more poignant knowing spirits were a reality on our plane of existence.

Dani stuck her head into the ladies' parlor where we'd set up our living room. Kota had artfully hidden the television inside a massive armoire we found upstairs. It made it easy to hide the modern device during tours which were starting next weekend. "What are you yelling about? Please tell me we don't have another ghost moving in."

I chuckled while Cami furrowed her forehead. "Why would you ask that? Lia gave no indication she was talking about a ghost."

I squeezed Cami's shoulders in a half hug. "It's a line from a movie. We'll have a *Ghostbusters* marathon one night soon. I was referring to a call I just got from another new client. His name is Albar, and he was referred by Stacia."

Dani cocked her head to the side. "Stacia is the shifter that asked us to throw her parents a fiftieth wedding anniversary next month, and Stacia is the one we saved from the skin-walker, right?"

"You are correct. I told you, your memory is just fine," I replied. Ever since our father was diagnosed with Alzheimer's we all worried when we forgot things. "He'd like us to come down and talk to him at his office in the business district. He wants to have an event next week."

The Central Business District (CBD) was a few blocks from the French Quarter and home to the high rises and big companies in NOLA. It surprised me to hear a supernatural worked among so many mundies. I shouldn't have been shocked. We'd encountered paranormals everywhere.

Dani shook her head from side to side. "We can't possibly add another event right now. We have the second line parade, and tours start next week. This will be too much."

Dre crossed her arms over her chest. "We can't afford to turn anyone away right now. The parade isn't happening here. Cami and I are finishing the parasols and the picture for the sign. We received confirmation from the brass band and have the beads. The route will be easy to walk through. There's not much else to do for that. There are four of us working full-time on the business. This is doable."

Dani sighed and gave Dre a small smile. "I know you're right. I'm allowing this mess with Marie and my relationship with Noah to add to my stress. It's those things that are over-whelming me, not the events. This new start was supposed to be easy and uncomplicated."

I sympathized with Dani. It was easy to allow personal issues to get in the way of work, especially when the issues were as big as the ones we were facing. One lesson I had learned when I lost Leo was that I couldn't allow my stuff to immobilize me and stop me from doing my job.

Life didn't stop for anything. You had to roll with the punches, get up and limp through no matter what because you had at least one person relying on you. With age and experience came the ability to suck it up, shove shit aside, and get what you needed to get done. There would be another day for us to deal with the rest of the crap.

And honestly, I was grateful for the reprieve. It would be easier to throw ourselves into the events rather than wonder when and where we might be attacked or how our lives were going to change, yet again, because we were Fated Ones.

"Have you not been paying attention for the past couple of decades. Life has never been easy and uncomplicated," I pointed out. "At least now you don't have your shifts at the hospital."

Dani grabbed her purse. "You can both stop. I get it. I'm done whining. Let's go. We can pick up some of that chicken Noah got me on the way back. I could use some comfort food."

I chuckled and stuffed my feet into my boots. "Sounds good to me. Is there anything we need to pick up for the parade on the way home?"

Dre picked up the iPad and opened Ava's file. "Nope. We have all of the parasols and will get those finished up while you're gone. Steve picked up the picture of her mom to add to the sign and we have everything to make the sashes."

Saying our goodbyes, Dani and I headed to the business district. Dani input the address into the GPS in my car. "This building is close enough that we can park at Ricky's parking lot if you want. It'll be easier than trying to find somewhere else."

"Maybe he'll even give us a discount now that we're part of the pack," I joked.

Dani snorted. "I don't think that's one of the perks of being a Fated One. So did Albar say what he'd like us to do for him?"

I shook my head as I drove down the freeway, glad it was late enough we were missing rush hour. "Just that he'll pay the extra fee for an expedited date."

"Let's hope he doesn't want us to plan a wedding," Dani replied. "Doing one in a week will be impossible unless all he wants is a barebones basic event."

I tapped my fingers on the steering wheel as I navigated the exit and headed to the parking garage. "We have enough on hand that we could pull off a better wedding than you think. It might not be one of our best, but it'd be better than most locations offer and you know it."

Dani lifted one shoulder. "The Six Twisted Sisters have a reputation to live up to. We don't do half-assed."

"No, we don't." I rolled down my window as I pulled up to Ricky.

The tall black shifter leaned his arm above my window. "Hello, ladies. What brings you down here today?"

I returned his smile and extended my credit card to him. "We have a meeting with a client, Albar. He's a broker in one of the high rises in the CBD."

Something crossed Ricky's green eyes but it was gone too fast for me to decipher what it was. "Yeah, he's a gargoyle. Good guy." He pushed my hand back inside the car. "No charge for you two. Park right here close to the booth."

Dani smirked at me. "Maybe you have the same power as Kota. That discount is even better than you hoped."

Ricky looked between us. "What am I missing?"

My laugh was strained as heat filled my cheeks. "I told her maybe we'd get a discount since we're part of the pack now. I was only joking. We aren't parking for free. You have a living to make, too."

Ricky raised one eyebrow and pointed to the spot beside the booth where he sat. "Pack does park for free. We take care of our own. No arguing."

Giving up on trying to pay, I pulled into the spot he pointed out and rolled my window up. "That'll come in handy since we seem to come down here several times a week to meet with clients."

Dani jumped out of the car and met me at the back of the car. "You can say that again. Thank you, Ricky. We owe you."

He shook his head. "No, you don't. I'll see you when you're done."

Giving him a nod and a wave, Dani and I headed in the opposite direction from the Quarter. A block and a half later we had glass and steel structures towering over us like giants. The sidewalks were crammed with mundies in suits going about their daily business. They were all hyper-focused on their work and oblivious to their surroundings.

We reached the office tower where Albar worked and piled into the elevator with a dozen people dressed for the occasion. I was painfully aware that Dani and I stuck out like a sore thumb in our jeans and sweaters. We made it to the thirty-eighth floor after a small eternity of stops.

A young twenty-something greeted us with too much cheer when we stopped and told her we were there for a meeting with Albar. "Can I get either of you anything to drink?" She asked as she showed us to his office.

I smiled at her. "No, thank you."

She nodded then knocked on the door to an office that had a plaque with Albar's name glued to the outside. She opened without waiting to get a response. "Mr. Jones your ten thirty is here."

The biggest man I'd ever seen got up from a fancy leather chair behind a mahogany desk. "Ah, yes. You must be two of the Six Twisted Sisters. Thank you for coming on such short notice."

The receptionist left Dani and I with the big guy. He had a square jaw and straight nose and shoulders the width of a small car. The dark pinstripe suit he was wearing had to have been custom made because no man looked like this guy did. He made Thor look emaciated in comparison.

If Ricky hadn't told me he was a gargoyle, I never would have guessed. Especially given his size. He was nothing like the small squat stone creatures perched on buildings. Maybe his slate eyes would have clued me in. It was hard to know what I would have thought without having the information beforehand.

One thing I knew with certainty, this was a powerful man in both the magical and mundane worlds. The energy I felt pulsing all around him made me want to learn more about gargoyles.

I extended my hand. "Yes, I'm Dahlia, we spoke on the phone. And this is my sister, Dani. What can we do for you?"

His hand completely engulfed mine. And his body temperature was only a couple of degrees cooler than the devil's ass crack. "I'd like you to throw me a cocktail party next Thursday night."

I fought not to shake my hand to cool it off when he released me. Dani's gasp was audible and she coughed to cover it up. "Sorry, um, I wasn't expecting it to be so soon. However, given that we have the night free, it won't be a problem. Tell me more about what you'd like. Is there a particular theme you would like? Do you want it held at Willowberry? And is this event for paranormals only, mundies only, or a mix of the two?"

I smiled at my sister. She managed to hide any shock over his grip wonderfully. Albar gestured to the chairs opposite his desk. "I'm not entirely sure what theme I'd like but I know I want it at your plantation. I keep hearing wonderful things about your set-up. This is a thank you to my co-workers for a record-breaking quarter."

I sat in the chair in front of me and inclined my head. "Given that, we should plan for a party involving mundies. Would you like this to be a formal affair? Or more informal?"

Albar leaned back in his chair and crossed his hands over his stomach. "Is there an in-between choice? While my colleagues might enjoy dressing up as if they're walking down the red carpet at the Oscars, I won't."

Dani nodded in understanding and tapped the edge of the desk. "What about an upscale Manhattan theme? Or perhaps we go with classy costume cocktail party and do a Roaring Twenties take on it? Martinis of all kinds can comprise the drink menu and we can find a restaurant to serve hors d'oeuvres like canapes, caviar, ceviche and gougeres."

Albar's eyes grew wide as Dani spoke. I hoped she had a restaurant in mind because we never ate stuff like that, and I had no idea where to find it. "I love the idea of the Roaring Twenties. Everyone here will love the idea of finding a twenties relevant costume. I want elegant and tasteful."

"We can use the inside of the house and ask our contractor about rigging up a bookcase doorway leading to the parlor with the drinks and food. Orchids and candles scattered throughout? You mentioned the red carpet. While we don't have red, we do have runners. What about a maroon and gold color scheme? And we have bar height tables and chairs or regular ones. Which do you prefer?" Dani asked as she held her phone in hand with the notes app open.

I looked over at Dani when she said that. We had one style of tables and chairs. And how the hell were we going to rig up a bookcase to slide on rollers? Crap on a cracker I might kill her. What the hell was she thinking?

Albar shook his head as he pulled a folder from inside his jacket pocket. "Ava wasn't kidding when she said you guys were the best. I'll pay extra for the bar height tables and the bookcase entrance. This will be a night none of my colleagues will forget. There will be sixty to seventy-five people. If you can give me an idea of the cost, I'll give you the deposit now. And I'll pay the entire fee for the short timeframe."

I cleared my throat and pulled out my phone to send Phi a text message. We needed to buy new tables and chairs and get Lucas and Noah to create a rolling bookcase. I gave her as many details as possible and asked her to come up with an estimate including a fee for short notice bookings as soon as she could.

I lifted a hand. My heart raced and I was low-key panicking. "Couple of questions before we can give you an estimate. Do you have a preference for the type of bartender? We've worked with Brezok in the past and I think he could be a good fit for a theme like this. Once you decide that, we need to know if you prefer to pay that person directly for the alcohol or if you'd like to make it a cash bar for your guests. And do you want us to handle all the food decisions? Or would you like to do that? Our clients do it both ways. If we handle these items, we need a budget for each, so we know what we are working with."

Asking those questions relaxed me quite a bit. There would be little customization, so these issues weren't insurmountable. We could rent tables if we had to.

"I'll leave the details up to you guys. I love everything you're thinking. Do you think ten grand is enough to cover the bar for the night for that many people without running out?" The gargoyle was worried ten thousand dollars wouldn't be enough? Was he serious?

"I don't want my guests paying for their drinks. As for

food, I'll make those arrangements with Restaurant R'evolution and have them deliver the food to the plantation. We usually go there at the end of the quarter, but I wanted to do something different this time," Albar continued. "I'm fine with Brezok as long as he doesn't enrapture any mundies."

Dani paused in entering notes on her phone. "Brezok agreed not to use his demonic powers on any of our clients or their guests while at Willowberry, so that won't be a concern. I'd like to style the décor around a sign of this woman that we cut out on our laser to hang in the room."

Dani showed Albar an image of a woman dressed in a long gown with a feather band in her hair. She was very elegant in a gown made of black and gold diamond shapes. It would take several hours to hand paint but seemed exactly what he wanted.

The smile that spread across Albar's face was brilliant. "That is beautiful and perfect. I'm going to have to keep a standing appointment with you guys every quarter for this event. The restaurant will never do again. I can't wait to see the look on everyone's face."

My phone pinged with a text and I showed Dani the figure Phi had given us. There was a reason we had Phi handle this part of the business. Dani and I would do this for half the cost and end up in the hole if it were up to us.

The thought of asking him for so much money turned my stomach. "The sister that handles the payment and invoices has let me know she will send an email to you so all you have to do is click the link and pay the deposit. She also indicated the budget for alcohol should be sufficient. I just need your email address."

Dani shifted in her seat as he gave me the details and I sent them to Phi. Dani cleared her voice a second later. "Phi also indicated that she will create an invitation using the image of the woman and send it to you, as well. The last detail we need to iron out is music. Would you like a band or DJ? The costs for those vary, and given the short notice, we might not be able to get a band. She will let you know when she sends the invoice."

"I'd prefer a jazz band but will settle for a DJ. Next time we will have more time. Although, you guys have more than met what I expected. I can't believe how much you can accomplish in such a short time," Albar remarked. "Especially, with Marie Leveau coming after you every other day."

My blood froze and the warm, happy feelings I had a moment before vanished. "We do our best."

Albar stood up, signaling the end of the conversation. "Well, your best can't be beat. I look forward to seeing what you create."

We shook hands again, then he gave each of us his card and we left. I immediately texted Phi about the band so she could make some calls, then looked up tables and chairs for rent and purchase. I was surprised at our options.

"How many tables do you think we need? Twenty? If we use the men's parlor, we can open the doors to the dining room and use both rooms. That'll be enough space," I told Dani as soon as we got to the sidewalk.

Dani nodded as she maneuvered around some people. "We will likely have to rent them this time. But we should look into investing, especially if he will be having us do a party every quarter. I'm calling Noah to ask about the hidden door idea."

I searched through the internet for tables and chairs while she talked to Noah. Based on her side of the conversation and the fact that she wasn't scowling, I took it that he said he could make the bookcase doors.

There was a bounce to her step when she finally hung up. This was the Dani I loved to see. "He said it wouldn't take him and Lucas long to create the doors at all. He's going to make them like he does barn doors, so we can leave them up if we want. I actually think it's a brilliant idea. It'll work well with the large foyer and be unique."

I couldn't help but smile with her. "He really was made for you. Aren't you glad we got the call, now?"

She pulled me into a hug. "Yes, I am. I haven't said this enough lately, but thank you for believing in my vision, and being willing to go all in with me. I love you, sestra."

I squeezed her tight as tears burned the backs of my eyes. "I love you, too."

She released me and started laughing. "Do you think Albar turns into a stone creature and fights demons? Or lives perched on a church somewhere?"

I laughed at that. "You sound like Dakota. I have no idea. Next time we will have to ask him."

Having another laundry list of shit to do helped keep both of us occupied so neither of us returned to fretting over the Voodoo Queen or being a Fated One.

CHAPTER 14

I stopped walking when I saw Noah walking through the tunnel between the main house and the original kitchen. A smile spread over his face as he headed right for me. Lucas was with him, but I barely noticed.

DANIELLE

Noah scooped me into his arms and kissed me senseless. My arms wound around his neck and I groaned when his tongue slid inside my mouth to tangle with mine. The man's lips should be registered as a lethal weapon. I was a puddle of desire by the time he broke away.

"It's nice to see you, too," I teased.

He grunted and set me on my feet. "I can't help how much I miss you when we're apart. Are you ready to make this door with me?"

I loved that he'd already gotten to know me so well. It helped that he wasn't afraid of hard work. "I can't wait. I found some designs on my go-to websites but wasn't sure if you already had a plan."

"We're going to alter our barn door design by adding sides and shelves," Lucas interjected.

Dahlia was wrapped in his arms with a goofy smile on her face. "I have the woman's face ready to cut out for the parade, but I'd like to help if possible. I've never made barn doors before."

"Do you know how to use a table saw?" Lucas asked.

Lia and I looked at each other then she patted his stomach. "Like a pro. I usually do all the cutting while Dani does the sanding. The drum sander has made that job a helluva lot easier."

Dre and Cami came out of our storage barn. Dre lifted her hand. "We found enough tables in stock at the resale warehouse, but the investment will be significant right now. It'll save us in the end, especially if Albar will be a regular customer."

Lucas and Noah narrowed their eyes. "Albar the gargoyle?"

I lifted my shoulder. "Yeah. Why? Ricky got a funny look when we told him. What's wrong with Albar?"

Noah dropped his head and looked at me through his lashes. The agony in his gaze made my stomach clench. "Gargoyles are the only creatures that can negate a mating."

What exactly did that mean? I could think of several interpretations for that statement. "I don't understand. I thought you said nothing could break our bond."

Noah sucked in a breath. "Nothing changes for the shifter. However, if you were to mate me and later you wanted a way out then Albar can dissolve your end of our connection."

Their reaction made sense given that information. I

twined my fingers with his. "Thank you for not keeping that from me. I can't imagine you like me knowing. Particularly, when I've already gone through two divorces. You have no reason to believe me, but I will not do that to you. I don't plan to mate you unless I am in this for the long haul. I had hoped that each of my marriages would last and that we'd grow old together. It didn't last because they didn't treat me right. I left because I deserve better. And so far, you're perfect."

Noah smiled at me then turned to Dre. "I didn't mean to sidetrack your discussion. If it's money you need to purchase the tables and chairs, we can help and you can pay us back later. Buying will save you a lot of money in the long run. And it could even make you money if you decide to ever rent them out yourselves."

I shook my head. "No, we can afford to spend the money now. You and Lucas have done enough to save us with the roof repairs and all the work you're doing around here."

"If we can't pay the mortgage or buy food, we will let you know," Dre teased. "I'll go put in the order with the resale warehouse so we can pick them up this weekend and have time if any need to be refinished."

Lia waved a hand in my direction. "There's no question of if, but when. You know Dani is ten steps ahead and has plans to chalk paint and wax them, or something."

I gasped and clutched my chest. "You wound me, Lia. I'd never chalk paint something we are using for upscale cocktail parties. We will be stripping them then sanding, sealing, staining, and finishing them."

Dre laughed and shook her head. "When are those shifters of yours coming to stay here?"

"I'll have them here in the morning ready to work. Are you thinking of finishing with an oil, lacquer, or polyurethane?" Lucas asked.

"Poly for sure. Lacquer is too thin for repeated use at

parties. We need the best protection against discoloring and scratches possible," Lia replied before I could.

"Let's use one of the marine polyurethanes. That eco-friendly one Phi found when she made her kitchen table." As a biological sciences professor at Tulane, Phi helped us remain as kind to the environment as possible. "The help will be welcomed because we can do them all at once and store them in one of the empty buildings to avoid ruining the finish while it dries."

Noah placed a quick kiss to my lips. "We have some marine varnish in our supplies. It might not be enough but we can grab some more. Let's get a workstation set up so we can get going."

"Usually, it's Dani cracking the whip," Dre teased Noah. "I'll get the tables ordered."

Lia crossed to Cami before she could follow Dre inside the house. "Cami, can you watch the laser after I set this design to run? I want to help with the bookcase doors."

"Sure. Is there anything I can paint while I'm waiting? I have to have something to do while the laser does its thing," Cami replied.

Lia headed for the silo where we had our customization machines and was telling her how we were going to paint the sign. I turned to Noah and clapped my hands together. "We have our table saw and miter saw on rolling stands. I can bring them out of the back barn and set them up outside unless you wanted to work under the covered area here."

Noah tugged me toward his truck. Lucas was already grabbing stuff out of the back. "We brought our miter saw and won't need a table saw. We cut the pieces of walnut for the backs before we left. We shouldn't need to run any other pieces, but we can grab your table saw if we do."

Emotion burned in my chest. Hugo helped me with some projects over the years, but more often than not I was calling my sisters and brothers for help with whatever I was doing. Hugo didn't like to be bothered and my first husband never did a damn thing.

"I don't know what I did to deserve you, but I couldn't be happier. Doing projects like this is my favorite thing in the world. I would have redone my house ten times over the years if I'd had the support."

Noah handed me a box containing the smaller electric tools we would need then grabbed a large pile of wood. "I will do anything you want. Building stuff is more than a job for me. Lucas, too. I've never had anyone other than him at my side, so this is going to be foreplay for me."

A laugh burst from me as we dropped our load in the tunnel. "This should be interesting."

Within no time we had the truck unloaded and several pairs of sawhorses set up. We followed Lucas inside to measure the double doors to the men's parlor. "We can do this a couple of ways. If we put them outside, we will need to join the two so they move together on the tracks. There isn't enough space between the front doors and the parlor opening for the left panel to slide toward the front of the house." Lucas pointed out the inadequate space.

"The wall to the right is long enough that both panels can slide that direction. And you won't have to move the pictures. The rail will hang them far enough away from the wall. The same applies if we hang them inside, but there you will need to move furniture and we will need to hang a new frame that is wide enough to cover the gap the rail makes." Lucas held his hands about six inches apart which I assumed was the depth of the potential gap we would have without a new door frame.

This one was a no-brainer to me. "They need to be hung outside of the parlor. That's how I envisioned it in my head."

We got to work taking measurements then went back

outside where Lia was organizing the wood by type. "I figured it would be easier to do this if we were organized." Her cheeks pinkened as she looked at Lucas.

Phi kept us organized while Dahlia was the one to figure out the cuts we needed to make. I approached Lia and showed her the list of measurements we'd taken. "We can get the measurements for the design details on the side and back panel after we have the base constructed, don't you think?"

Lia looked at the numbers for a few seconds, then jotted down the lengths she thought we'd need for the crossbar and frame for each. "Let's start with putting the walnut pieces together to create the back panel so we can run it through the belt sander. We will need four and not quite a half."

I turned to grab what we needed and noticed Lucas and Noah staring at each other. I winced when I realized Lia and I had taken over. "Sorry. Where do you guys want to start?"

Lucas laughed and kissed the top of Lia's head. "I like the way my lady thinks. I have the Kreg jig over here."

Together we drilled pocket holes then placed the pieces of walnut together on the sawhorses and screwed them together. With that done, Noah lifted the first back panel and leaned it against the house. "I'll take them both to the barn to sand them down while you guys work on the frames. But for now, I will sand these individual pieces."

Having Noah and Lucas there to help, made the project easy and fun. Neither of them tried to tell us how to use the power tools. Nor did they take over when we were doing something.

Lucas and Lia worked seamlessly cutting the angles for the frames and before long we had one of the back panels ready to stain. I took that job while Noah sanded the boards and they finished attaching the frame to the second panel.

By the time Dre and Steve came over we were working on attaching the crossbars to the backs to give it some decorative details on the side that would be seen from inside the room. Dre crouched down next to me. "You know you guys could have taken off the existing doors and used them."

"I considered that, but the shelves wouldn't have attached flush to the panels. Instead, we will repurpose them in one of the other buildings out back," I told her.

Cami joined us a bit later and let us know she'd already painted the pieces for the sign and cut out everything Lia had asked, so she watched as we continued cutting and applying the cross bars to the pieces.

Assembly was fast after that thanks to the summer heat speeding up the drying process. Noah grabbed a wooden dowel and handed it to me. "We need to fill the pocket holes so they aren't visible behind the books on the shelves."

I looked at the small round stick and the holes. "I've never actually done this part. I haven't made something like this where both sides will be visible before."

Noah's eyes widened a fraction. "You mean I get to teach you something?"

"What can I say? It's your lucky day," I preened.

He laughed and showed me how to insert the dowel so it was flush, then using a small saw to cut off the excess. Wood glue seeped out around the piece that was now flush with the panel. Because I had already stained the piece, the fix was obvious. It wouldn't stay that way for long, though.

I teased Noah and he gave it right back to me as we worked on finishing the bookcase doors. By the time we were done with that part and ready to go inside, I'd managed to fall harder for the sexy shifter.

There was a smile in my heart and on my face. I couldn't remember the last time I'd had this much fun with a guy I was dating. My sisters and I laughed and had a blast doing just about everything, but I couldn't say the same about both of my ex-husbands.

I had no idea that this was missing all these years. Having this with a romantic partner, as well as my sisters, filled a void in me that had been there a very long time. It was both exhilarating and terrifying. Feeling so whole gave me too much to lose if things between Noah and I went bad.

I had to give myself a mental headshake as we entered the house to hang the hardware above the doors. I had to stop the negative thinking. There was no reason to borrow trouble.

CHAPTER 15

DAHLIA

"The route goes from Chartres, across Conti, and down Bourbon so we pass Lafitte's Blacksmith bar because Ava's mom worked there for years," Phi explained as we walked through the Quarter.

It was packed with tourists, even this early in the day, thanks to the summer months. That was the reason Ava chose now to honor her mom. Apparently, Ava's mom loved the hustle and bustle of the Quarter during peak times which was one reason she worked at the popular bar for so long.

I looked around taking in the sights and sounds around us. Dani was finishing up the big sign of the woman for Albar's party and finding books in the house to put on the shelves that were currently curing. Dre, Cami, and Kota were helping her.

"Have you talked to Dea lately? I'm worried about her." I hoped Phi knew more. She was the one of us that was closest to Dea. Phi was the baby of the family and Dea was right above her in the family line.

Phi gave me a sideways look. "She hasn't returned my calls. She's been working her four nights this week, so I'm sure that's why. This whole ghost business has taken its toll on her but she's going to be fine. She's a strong woman."

Phi's reassurances did little to ease the band of worry around my chest. I couldn't explain it, but it felt like Dea was barely hanging in the balance right now. "It hasn't been easy for her at all. Still, we should check on her later if she doesn't stop by."

Phi smiled at me as she nudged my shoulder. "That's a great plan. Did you get a chance to see the DJ choices for Albar's party? I couldn't find any bands available on such short notice."

"I liked all of them. I say we let him decide. These evites are something else, sestra. How did you manage those so fast? I thought we would have to ask Mackenna to do something in photoshop for us." My daughter Mackenna was a graphic designer and did work for us all the time. Phi and I both could manage some basic stuff with some of the programs, so we did what we could without having to ask Mack for help, given how busy she was lately.

Phi waved a hand through the air. "It was easy with Canva. I used the picture Dani downloaded from our stock photo account as the background. You know how easy it is to add layers in that program. A little glitter, and the details, and it was done. It barely took me fifteen minutes."

"You're getting good at navigating that program, and it shows. Albar was over the moon about the invitations and is actually having them printed to hand out to his team," I informed her.

Phi sucked air through her teeth. "I hope they print well. Mack is always telling me to pay attention to CMYK or something when an image needs to be printed, and I didn't do that."

I chuckled having had similar conversations with my daughter. "I can never remember what color schemes don't print well. I did mention that and told him to let me know if he runs into any problems. He's incredibly impressed with the progress we made in a day and is spreading the word about us."

"We could use the business at Willowberry. Not that we've struggled to pay the mortgage and bills. We've actually been in the black. This will be the first event where we go in the red because of the tables, but not by much."

I lost track of what Phi was saying when I noticed a shimmer in the air ahead of us as we turned onto Conti Street. I grabbed Phi's arm and pulled her to the side. "Do you see that?"

Phi scanned the street with a frown. "No, oh holy shit. What is it?"

"I don't know," I hissed as I pulled her closer to the anomaly. There were fewer tourists here but still too many. "But it's clearly supernatural. It could be a ghost maybe."

Phi shook her head from side to side. "I don't think so. It's almost like a dark-colored rainbow."

My heart stopped, my vision swam, and I was assailed by the smell of fried green tomatoes and remoulade. It was a scent I'd inhaled thousands of times but never like this. Dizziness made me stumble, and my legs gave out.

My knees hit the sidewalk as the smell overwhelmed me. "No," I whispered as the familiar sensation of being pulled into a vision came over me.

My vision wavered, and the sight of Phi and my surroundings disappeared, but not before I saw tiny red-skinned devils jumping on Phi. They had tiny horns and long tails with a spade at the end, like every cartoon caricature I'd ever seen. My heart raced, and my mind whirled as I tried to remain in the present to help my sister.

My attempts did nothing but give me a headache and disorient me for several seconds too long. When I stopped fighting the process, I saw Lucinda with a different woman strapped to a table. This woman had dark brown hair and eyes. There was something similar about her, but I couldn't figure out what.

The wooden structure served as an altar on a ritual space that looked a lot like what we'd cleansed at her home. The table wasn't the only clue that it wasn't the same place. The symbols on the floor and walls had a sheen to them as if they were fresh, and the space wasn't as dark and dank, despite the walls and floor being made of stone this time. It was almost as if the dark energy hadn't had time to erode the natural energy around her.

Lucinda hadn't changed, though. She had on the ceremonial robe with the dagger in her hand. She was chanting something in a foreign language. There were others with her in the room, but they hung back. Their energy made my skin prickle. I expected their voices to join in the ceremony, but they remained silent.

As Lucinda's chant grew in tenor, candles, and torches came to life, and she danced around the table and the terrified woman. When Lucinda reached the victim's left side, she plunged the weapon into her chest.

Blood spurted from the wound when Lucinda withdrew the dagger. Bile filled the back of my throat as I watched Baron Samedi peel away from the group surrounding them and float into the woman on the table.

It hit me, as I watched the possessed woman sit up and smile, that we hadn't stopped anything. Not yet, at least. The woman had a dark purple glow surrounding her as she got unsteadily to her feet. Black blood dribbled out of the side of her mouth as she smiled. I swear I could see Samedi's skeletal image over her face.

Lucinda then approached the people lurking in the shadows around them. "Come feed your god and give him the sustenance he needs to live." Instinct told me these individuals were mundies. I looked back at the victim to determine why she felt different when it hit me. She had to be a witch. That was why she felt familiar to me.

One by one people moved toward the possessed woman. What happened next horrified me. Samedi used the woman to consume the mundies. The possessed witch held their faces and lowered her face to them like she was going to kiss them. With their mouths an inch or two apart the possessed witch inhaled, and blue light drifted from the mundies and traveled into her. The Mundie's skin dried up and withered as they turned to dust at her feet.

My stomach roiled, and I once again found myself grateful that I couldn't smell anything in my visions. I was fairly sure it would smell like roadkill in this room at the moment.

The possessed witch's head snapped in my direction when I made a sound of disgust. That wasn't possible, was it? I was witnessing the future, so something in the direction of where I was standing must have caught her attention.

Before I could look around to get a better idea of where this ritual space was located, I was jerked back to reality to find one of the tiny demons pulling on my short white-blonde hair. "What the actual?"

I reached up to grab the asshole. My hand wrapped around a leg that felt like leather, and it bit me. My reactions were slowed thanks to the effects of coming out of a vision.

A few feet from me Phi was fighting a dozen of the red demons while trying to get to me. She had cuts all over her body and looked like she'd wrestled a wild boar. Her clothes were filthy and there was a straw sticking out of her hair along with what looked like a used condom.

I grunted as I pushed myself to my hands and knees. The tiny demon on my head slid sideways and hung from a section of braided hair. Part of my mind noted I hadn't fared much better than my sister. Although, I surmised my face hurt thanks to impact with the sidewalk.

My movement caught the attention of several of the ones attacking Phi, and they raced toward me. I remained on my knees, not trusting my legs to hold me up. I wrapped my fingers around one skinny, red leg, then yanked the demon off my hair, pulling several strands with it.

I snarled at the creature dangling from my grip. "Are you alright, Phi?"

Phi's gaze snapped in my direction. Her shoulders sagged, and she sighed. "Lia, thank God you're alright. I was so worried. Are you hurt?"

I tossed the demon against the wall next to us and punched one of the others coming at me. I was lucky that I managed to do anything with how weak I felt at the moment. It usually took me a few to steady myself after a vision. "Not as hurt as you. My right cheek might be fractured, but nothing Kip can't fix."

A growl left Phi as she tried to buck the four tiny creatures holding down her arms. "I'm so sorry. I couldn't help you."

"You have nothing to be sorry for." I yelped when teeth sunk into my calf. My leg jerked and kicked out instinctively. Unfortunately, that didn't faze the demon. Before I could blink, I had half a dozen swarming me. "Where did all the mundies go?"

"The ones that were on the street with us hurried away when the shimmer appeared, and none have ventured down this street in the past five minutes or so. It hasn't been long," Phi said through clenched teeth.

I crawled toward her, making the demons clinging to me come along for the ride. I couldn't move too fast because my mind was still swimming from the vision. The claws and teeth that were embedded in me tore at my skin. Once I reached Phi's side, I pushed the demons closest to me off of her arm.

Phi came up swinging with a shout. I turned my attention to the ones trying to push me to the sidewalk. These things sounded like a pack of hyenas. They laughed, yelled, squeaked, and whooped as they pummeled, bit, and scratched us.

Oddly enough, the demons seemed to be holding back. I sensed they had more power than they were using which made little to no sense. I filed that away to consider later. "Do you think Leveau sent them after us?" I asked Phi.

Phi's gaze snapped in my direction. "Do you think that's possible? I thought her powers were tied to a different pantheon of gods."

"They are," a male voice replied.

The tiny demons shrieked and scrambled away from us at the same time Phi and I both turned to check out our newcomer. It was the UIS agent we'd met at Lucinda's house the other day.

My heart leaped in my chest when I caught sight of the well-dressed guy in the suit. "Xinar. Can you help us stop these things? We can't let them get away."

Xinar said something in a foreign language that froze the demons closest to him. The others took off, scurrying up the side of the building where they disappeared. He cursed and raced into the courtyard where many of the demons had gone.

Phi got up and helped me to my feet. I wobbled as I

moved to check the frozen devil in front of us. It hung in the air mid-leap with one leg lifted higher than the other and its arms reaching ahead of its body.

I jumped when the creature yelped after I poked it in the side. "Sweet baby, Jesus. How did he do that?"

Phi shook her head and waved a hand in front of another demon. "I'm not sure. Who is he?" Her comment trailed off when we heard a screech in the courtyard.

I turned and ran hoping Xinar was alright. "He's one of Aidoneus's UIS agents."

When we reached him, Xinar had a dagger dripping blood in his hand and a dead demon at his feet. "The rest got away," he told us as he stowed the blade in the inside pocket of his suit jacket.

"What are they?" I asked as Phi, and I followed him to the street where the devils were still frozen.

Xinar pulled something from a pocket and touched it to the first demon's head making it disappeared. "They're imps. Lower-level demons that thrive on chaos. They've become more popular in this realm, ever since Aidoneus and his mate constructed the first Hellmouth months ago."

I gestured to Phi. "This is the baby of the family, Delphine."

"Nice to meet you, Delphine." Xinar inclined his head in her direction then continued making the remaining imps disappear.

Phi cleared her throat. "You, as well. What is a Hellmouth? And why are these imps popular?"

I lifted a hand. "Who brought them here? Was it Leveau? Phi thinks her power is different."

Xinar chuckled as he smoothed the front of his suit. "A Hellmouth is a gate connected to a field that prevents demons from crossing to this realm. It also makes it harder for witches to conjure them to do their bidding. The imps are popular because bringing them forth takes less energy than it does to bring one of the higher-level demons. You are right, Phi. This was not Leveau. It was a Tainted witch wanting imps to do her dirty work for her."

I'd heard Kaitlyn mention Tainted witches but I didn't have a good grasp on what that meant. "I've heard that term before. What exactly does it mean?"

Xinar started walking down Conti, and we followed beside him. "Tainted witches are those that have stolen magic from other beings in order to gain more power. They use questionable spells and often go Dark when they stoop to using Blood magic to gain more power."

Phi pursed her lips. "What you're saying is that we have some Tainted witch in the area conjuring demons to help her get more powerful?"

Xinar inclined his head. "Precisely."

I rubbed my temples as we walked. "That's just what we need right now. Nullifying the ritual space didn't stop Lucinda. I just saw her killing a witch so Baron Samedi could take control of her body."

Xinar cursed. "Are things here always this chaotic?"

Phi and I looked at each other and shrugged. "Don't ask us. We've only been in the magical world a few months," I replied.

I had hoped we stopped Lucinda and Marie from completing their plans to bring the loa to this realm. Unfortunately, I was wrong. This new vision gave me limited information as to where they planned this ritual this time. I wasn't sure how many locations had stone chambers, but we needed to find out.

CHAPTER 16

DAHLIA

Xinar's focus shifted to Phi and me. "You six already have quite the reputation for being bad asses. I must admit that I didn't believe the rumors when I heard them. I thought surely someone had it wrong. When Aidoneus confirmed his mate recently did something to activate your magic, I was floored. How is it that you are skilled enough to stop a skin walker and a siren from returning one of their own to the fold?"

Phi patted him on the shoulder with a smile. "We're awesome like that. But seriously, we credit our mother. The way she lived her life taught us that we could do anything we put our minds to."

The hole that was left in my heart when our mom died ached and throbbed painfully. It took a long time for me to see the full scope of my mom's strength, determination, and grace. She never gave up on a goal, no matter how long it took.

I was so proud of my mother for finally getting her high school diploma when I graduated from the university with my Master's Degree in Social Work. The way she held her head high and celebrated was inspirational.

That was a couple of decades before she was diagnosed with stage four inflammatory breast cancer. The prognosis wasn't good when they caught it, but she fought with everything she had and lived for over two years after that.

I paused at the corner of Royal and Conti and grabbed Phi's arm. "We should get back to Willowberry and help finish what we can for Albar's party. We know the parade route and are ready for that event. This issue with Lucinda and the loa is going to blow up in our face if we don't find her soon and stop her."

Xinar had stopped with us and dipped his head. "That's the wisest course of action in my opinion. If I can be of any assistance, please let me know."

I cocked my head to the side. "Why are you helping us? Did Phoebe tell you to help us?"

Xinar's forehead narrowed on me. "Phoebe doesn't give me orders. My loyalty is to Aidoneus, and he assigned me to this area to help control the demon population. Although, I know both Aidon and Phoebe would want me to provide any assistance I can."

Phi tapped her lower lip with a finger as she considered Xinar. "How did you find us today? Maybe you can use that same magic to locate Lucinda."

"I would love to be able to use these powers to locate the mambo. However, not only are our magics from different pantheons, they are also keyed to different beings. I am only able to track and locate demons using magic. It's how I was able to get here before the imps disappeared," Xinar explained.

I frowned. "Does that mean that the Tainted witch conjured them to appear here?"

Xinar's eyes widened. "No, it doesn't. Demons appear in the circle where the magic is cast to call them through the veil. I felt the demonic energy traveling which is why it took time for me to get here. I had to wait until that energy came to a stop to lock onto their location."

"Do you know where the portal originated? Maybe we can locate the Tainted witch by going to that site," Phi said.

"I was just thinking the same thing," I agreed.

Xinar nodded as he gave Phi and I an appreciative look. "I am beginning to understand the reason you six are so controversial. You should be terrified of the evil in this world, and yet, you do not hesitate to jump in with both feet. I was planning on visiting the location where the imps were brought through. I will keep you posted should I find anything."

I looked at Phi. "Dinner?"

Phi nodded. "Definitely."

Xinar watched us with one eyebrow raised. I smiled and waved a hand through the air. "Sorry, sister shorthand. Would you be willing to come to Willowberry for dinner tonight? I am going to ask Kaitlyn to join us. You can update us on what you found, and we can talk about possible locations for this new space I saw Lucinda performing the ritual."

Xinar placed a hand over his lower abdomen and bowed slightly. "I will be there at six-thirty. And I will ask questions of my contacts to see if anyone has heard about Marie Leveau or her mambos relocating."

We said our goodbyes and went back to the car. Ricky was pacing next to my SUV and stopped when he saw us. "You're hurt. Were you two behind the portal I felt a bit ago? Lucas said you don't know how to open one, and asked me to go find you, but I couldn't leave the lot unattended. I'm pretty sure he's on his way here now."

I pulled my phone out and called Lucas. "Lia. Is everything okay? Ricky called when he felt the portal."

"Phi and I are both alright. There's a Tainted witch somewhere in the city that sent imps through a portal to Conti Street. Xinar arrived and dealt with the imps, but I had a vision in the interim. We're on our way back to Willowberry now if you want to join us there. Lucinda is still a problem," I explained. I should tell him about my cheek. The more I moved, the worse it got, but I didn't want to worry him.

"We will be there shortly. Do you want me to have Wynona meet us there?" His offer to have the pack healer join us let me know he sensed there were at least minor injuries. She had potions and tonics, but they wouldn't help heal a cracked bone.

"No, I'll give Kip a call. See you soon." I hung up before he could say anything else.

Phi plucked my keys from my hand and unlocked the doors. "I'll drive. At the rate your face is swelling, your vision will be compromised in no time."

I didn't argue with her. Mainly because my head was throbbing so I was happy to let someone else drive. I took the time to send Kaitlyn a message asking her to come over for dinner to discuss Lucinda.

After receiving her agreement, I pulled up Kip's number and hit the call button. The phone rang through the car's speakers. The healer answered on the third ring. "What can I do for you, Dahlia."

"Hello, Kip. Delphine is in the car with me. We're hoping you are available to treat some imp bites and claw marks, as well as a possible broken cheekbone."

The healer sucked in a breath. "I just finished up with a patient. Do you want to stop by? Or have me come to you?"

We weren't all that far from her house, but she might be helpful when we discuss Lucinda later. "Would you mind coming to Willowberry? As you probably know, we are trying to stop Lucinda Malum from giving the god Baron Samedi a body. We managed to neutralize the ritual space in her home, but I had another vision that showed she moved her work somewhere else. So Kaitlyn and Xinar, the Underworld Investigative Services agent, are coming for dinner to strategize. We could use your input, too."

"I will be there in half an hour. Since you are in the car, I feel I should warn you to get home as quickly as possible. Demon venom can cause numerous side effects, one of which is blurry vision."

Phi sighed as she pressed the gas pedal, speeding up. "Of course it is. Thanks for the warning."

Kip assured us she would be there and hung up. I glanced at Phi who was white knuckling the steering wheel. "We're going to make it home without any problems."

Phi snorted and shook her head. "Yeah, because we aren't lightning rods for every remote side effect on the planet. Mom took all of our luck where that is concerned." She held up a hand. "Not that I wouldn't have happily given the immunity to her. It would just be nice to have her luck with that now, you know what I mean?"

Delphine went through her own battle against breast cancer four years ago. After a radical double mastectomy, she had to have chemo and radiation. Since then, she had thankfully been cancer free. What she was referring to was the fact that our mom never suffered from crazy side effects during the two-plus years of treatment she endured. Phi was just as strong as our mom but had experienced most of the side effects.

I squeezed her shoulder. "I know exactly what you mean.

You're as strong as mom. And, because I know you won't complain, how are you feeling? Any dizziness?"

"I'm okay." The second the words were out of her mouth Phi and I both started laughing and crying. That was what mom said to us during the last few weeks of her life despite what had to be excruciating pain.

We spent the rest of the drive sharing stories about our mom. Lucas was waiting for me when we pulled up. It was nice to have him close after the emotional car ride home. He touched my cheek gently. "Let's ice this."

Phi waved to him. "Hello, Lucas."

He shifted his gaze to my sister and his frown deepened. "You both look like you've been through it this afternoon. Do we need to do a clean-up with the mundies?"

Phi shook her head. "The second the portal appeared the area cleared out. The only one that came across us after that was Xinar."

Lucas ran a hand over the back of his neck. "When is Kip going to be here?"

As if in answer to his question, the healer pulled up at that moment. "Right now," I said looking back from the tunnel. "Lucas, can you tell Dre and Kota that we are having guests for dinner? I need to know if we should order something. I'm in no shape to cook right now."

"I'll take care of it." Lucas pressed his lips to mine before he entered the back door.

Phi and I took seats in the outdoor seating area and waited for Kip. The healer winced as she set her bag on the table in front of us. "You two look like hell. But I see you made it without incident."

I gestured to Phi. "Heal her first. She got the brunt of the imp attack while I was out with my vision."

Phi shook her head as Kip pulled several potions and tonics from her bag. "Each of you drink one of these."

I grabbed the green vial. I hummed in approval when I smelled the fresh pineapple scent. Phi clinked her bottle with mine and we drank them down. Kip worked fast as she smeared a paste over some of Phi's wounds before using her healing magic.

I felt the warmth of the healer's power fill the air and smelled a fresh herbal scent. Delphine's bruises disappeared before my eyes. She rolled her head, cracking her neck before she smiled at Kip. "Much better. Thank you so much."

Kip inclined her head and shifted her focus to me. "This one is going to hurt." I winced when she probed my cheek.

I clenched my teeth and nodded. That healing heat surrounded me this time. It was accompanied by the same scent. It preceded the pain she warned me about. I hadn't felt pain when I injured the bone because I was sucked into a vision. That made the feel of a hot ice pick stabbing into my face even worse.

Thankfully, the white-hot agony vanished in under a minute. My breathing evened out, and my heart started slowing back to a normal rate. "You are a miracle worker. We owe you a party. If you ever want to have one here, just let us know."

Kip pursed her lips. "I'll take a personalized tumbler."

My eyes bulged. "You've got it. What do you want?"

"I've always wanted the coven to have a logo that we can use to brand ourselves. We're the biggest one in the world, and I think that deserves recognition," Kip explained.

A smile spread over my face. I loved the idea. "After we finish this battle with Lucinda, let's get with the others and come up with something."

"The coven might overwhelm you with ideas," Kip teased me.

I was laughing at her when Lucas came out of the house a

second later. He let me know that Noah and Dani were on their way to pick up the fried chicken and the fixings.

Kaitlyn and Xinar arrived while Noah and Dani were gone. Phi and Dre served everyone drinks while I updated the head witch on what had occurred earlier that afternoon. Kaitlyn's expression, as she looked at Xinar, was a cross between flirty and confused. "How is it that you managed to come across the sisters two days in a row?"

The smile Xinar gave Kaitlyn was one that would melt the panties of most women. He was dressed to impress in his suit, with his black hair perfectly styled. "I was tracking demonic power surges, and that is what led me to the sisters each time. Demons are drawn to the death magic and normally I could use that, but Marie hides the mambos too well."

Kaitlyn blushed under Xinar's attention. "Regardless of how well she is masking her mambos, she's overlooked one important factor. Demons are drawn to the magic Marie, and her crew are performing. That means eventually, during your normal duties, you will come across Lucinda."

Phi glared a Kaitlyn. "There's no way we can wait for that to happen. You've got to have a way to find the stone chamber. Otherwise, one of your witches is going to be killed and become host to Baron Samedi."

Kaitlyn sighed and ran a hand over the back of her neck. "You're right. The only place I can think of to search is Marie's lair in St. Louis Cemetery number one. When I accompanied Phoebe there, before the ritual at your plantation, I noted the place was stone. We can search there, but we need to create the potion we used to cleanse Lucinda's house. I'd like us to do it as a group. That way, we will have enough to distribute to the coven should they come across her in their own searches."

Dani and Noah arrived with dinner, and Kaitlyn brought

her up to speed while we got drinks, plates, and silverware for everyone. When we were all seated with food in front of us, Dani picked up a chicken leg but didn't take a bite. She stared at Kaitlyn for several seconds. "Do you really think it's wise to have witches using this potion without backup?"

I sucked in a breath thinking the head witch was going to get upset at being questioned. Instead, Kaitlyn turned her hand from side to side. "Yes and no. I will be advising everyone to use caution. However, I don't think we can take the chance if someone happens to run across her. As your sister pointed out, one of us is on the line. I don't take threats to my witches lightly."

"I'd like to make a suggestion," Dre interjected. "Dani makes a good point, so perhaps if Lucinda is found, they check in with you before acting. That way, we can determine how fast we can get to her and already be on our way before they do anything."

Kaitlyn nodded as she chewed a bite of creamed corn. "That's a reasonable plan. I'll even go one further and tell them to cloak themselves before they call me and remain that way unless it looks like Lucinda is going to move forward with the sacrifice."

Xinar added his opinion as the plan got more and more detailed. I participated, adding my two cents here and there, but for the most part, I sat and considered if Marie would truly have Lucinda doing this in her lair. She'd been adamant that she wasn't involved in our earlier attack and denied involvement with Lucinda's plan. It just seemed like a huge risk for her to take. My gut told me Lucinda was somewhere else.

CHAPTER 17

DANIELLE

Kota rubbed her hands together. "Let's get this potion made so we can find this bitch and make her regret trying to turn one of our kind into a loa's meat suit."

I raised my fist and bumped it with Dakota's. "She should know better by now than to underestimate the Twisted Sisters."

Kaitlyn chuckled from her position on the other side of the long wooden table we'd made for our magical kitchen. "I would agree with you. Word is getting around the magical world about your heritage and abilities. Most are thanking the gods for bringing you six. I wasn't so sure at first. I'm coming around. For the first time in my life, I've found the courage to stand up for all of magical kind like I have always wanted. When I got the position of head witch, my predecessor told me how it was my job to keep the witches in line and avoid pissing off Marie."

I sorted the jars of what we needed to make the potion. "It's got to be difficult to stand up to someone when you've grown up being taught that she was the queen of everything."

Kaitlyn inclined her head. "We're also told stories about what she and those that came before her have done to their enemies. No one wants to become one of her zombies. Or to become food for her wendigos."

One of Lia's eyebrows lifted to her hairline. "Wendigo? What's that?"

"They're cannibals of significant spiritual strength. They're gaunt to the point of emaciation with desiccated skin pulled taut over their bones. The wendigo looks like a gaunt skeleton recently disinterred from the grave. I've never seen one personally because Leveau only brings them out in dire situations. However, the stories claim its bones are pushing out against its skin, and it has a complexion the ash grey of death. I always thought the eeriest part were how its eyes are pushed back deep into their sockets and its lips are tattered and bloody," Kaitlyn explained.

A shudder worked its way down my spine. "Those sound terrible. Let's hope we don't drive her to sic those on us."

Dre narrowed her eyes and threw the herbs Kaitlyn had listed for us into her cauldron. "What are the chances of that? Why doesn't she use them more often?"

Kaitlyn held up a jar of herbs and poured some into her palm, showing us how much she had. "Because unlike her zombies, wendigos can't be controlled completely. They have minds of their own and have a tendency to be ruled by their hunger. They'll even turn on Marie. The legend about them says that she's had to kill them every time they've been brought out of wherever she holds them. Now add the fennel to the cauldron."

Phi grimaced as she did as she was instructed. "Let's hope

she doesn't decide to use them on us. After this is done, we should learn the wendigo weaknesses."

Kaitlyn picked up the next jar of herbs and poured it into her palm, showing us how much to add. "That's easy. Witch fire will incinerate them faster than anything else and keep you as far from their claws and teeth as possible. One scratch or bite turns you into one of them. Although, I'm told dragons are immune, so you six might be as well."

I smiled as I called my dragon side and turned my fingernails into talons. So far, I was the only one that had managed to shift part of my body. Lia tapped my hand, then looked at Kaitlyn. "Can we practice reaching that part of us, the next lesson? I want to see if the rest of us can shift at all."

Phi lifted a hand. "Or breathe fire. How cool would that be?"

We all chuckled. I added the next herb to my cauldron as pounding on the wall to our right made me smile. Noah and Lucas were adding a section to the magical kitchen that could serve as a bedroom or storage. "Stop mooning over the wolves and focus." Kaitlyn's voice snapped me back into the moment.

My cheeks heated as I focused on the head witch. "Sorry about that. Can you tell us about Tainted witches? As you know from Xinar there's one in the city that is summoning demons to our realm."

Kaitlyn blew out a breath as she showed us how much distilled water to add to the cauldron. "Like Xinar explained they're witches that steal power that doesn't belong to them. A Tainted witch can become a Blood witch or a Dark witch if they kill their victim and use their blood to cast spells. They turn Dark when they use forbidden spells that do something like suppress a person's will so they can force the witch to do their bidding."

Lia stirred her potion in the same slow manner as Kaitlyn. "Is there any way that we can locate them? We need to make sure they can't keep releasing demons in our city. The imps might not have been the most violent things we've faced, but they could hurt mundies and expose the magical world."

Kaitlyn shook her head from side to side. "Add the last ingredient and turn the heat down to a simmer. There's no way to find Tainted, Blood, or Dark witches without using forbidden spells. And even then, you aren't guaranteed to get a result. Scrying is the best method by which witches find anything. And to do that, we need something personal. Seeing as we have no idea who is doing this, I'm at a loss. I'm not sure who I can trust and who to suspect."

I frowned at the head witch. "What do you mean you don't know who to trust? Don't you know if a witch has turned?"

Kaitlyn lifted one shoulder. "That used to be the case. Or so we thought. Someone in Phoebe's circle discovered a spell to hide any darkness. I'm hoping she will have some advice on how to counter that spell soon. The alert she sent to all of the head witches indicated she was going to look into the issue further, but she's busy."

Smoke started billowing out of Dea's cauldron as she sat there looking down at the mixture. The smell of burning herbs turned my stomach while the smoke made my eyes burn and had all of us coughing.

Kaitlyn jumped into action and hurried over to Dea. She cast a spell making one of the windows open and blowing the thick smoke outside. "You had your heat too high, Dea. Let's get your cauldron cleaned and start over."

Dea scowled at Kaitlyn as she grabbed the cauldron off her stand and carried it to the sink in the traditional kitchen area Lucas and Noah had finished last week. They had included minimal cupboards along with a fridge, a range, and sink with disposal. They left out the island and the bulk of the cabinets to give us room for the potions work, but the space could be fully converted to a living space with minimal effort if needed.

I watched as Dea dropped the iron pot into the sink and started scrubbing it. I was shocked at her behavior and wondered how the hell she'd grabbed the thing when it had to be hot enough to burn her.

Lia gave me her we-should-talk-to-her look before she turned back to her own potion. Focusing on mine, I wondered how we would know it was done. "How will we know if we got it right?"

Kaitlyn's forehead was scrunched up when she turned from watching Dea. She shook her head and smiled. "You want a bright green liquid in your cauldron. It'll smell fresh as spring."

Mine was green, but it wasn't bright. I leaned over and cursed silently when it wasn't like she described. Kota whooped a second later. "I got it, sestras!"

Kaitlyn crossed to her and laughed when Dre fist-bumped her. "Very good, Dakota. Now use your baster and transfer it to as many vials as you can."

"Did I ruin mine?" I wanted to start over now if that was the case. I discovered I didn't really care for potion making. It was boring and took too much time for my taste. I wasn't surprised Kota had mastered it. She was one of the better cooks among us.

Kaitlyn took my spoon and stirred the mixture. "Did you add the fennel? I think you're missing that."

I couldn't recall if I had or not. I was too busy listening to her tell us about wendigos. "I don't think so. I wasn't paying close attention."

Kaitlyn pursed her lips, and I could tell she was struggling not to tell me something. I waved her on. "Go ahead and yell at me."

That made the head witch smile. "I don't want to yell at you, but I have to warn you and everyone else here that it is imperative that you pay close attention when you are mixing potions. Especially when it comes to imbuing them with magic at the end. Some of them can quite literally blow up in your face. Potion making can be a delicate matter."

My heart skipped a beat. "How do we know which ones will blow up? I have to admit this isn't my forte, and it's likely I will get distracted in the future, so I want to avoid the ones that can maim or kill me."

Kaitlyn moved to Dea's spot as she returned with her clean cauldron. The head witch poured the first herb into her palm. "Watch what I do and when I turn down the heat, Dea. As for potions, I would normally tell you guys that information can be found in your family grimoire, but since you are just starting yours that doesn't apply, so I will bring you several each time we practice and let you know which ones need extra caution."

"Thanks. We would seriously be lost without you," I told her honestly.

Dre lifted her hand. "I think I got mine. It looks and smells like Kota's."

Kaitlyn checked Dre's and nodded. "Very good. We have enough to hand out to a couple of dozen witches. They're ready to patrol as soon as the sun goes down. We should have enough to give everyone a vial."

Lia lifted her wooden spoon. "Can you check mine? And are they ready to call you before they act?"

Kaitlyn brought the spoon to her nose. "That's perfect, Lia. Everyone is aware of the order to call me, and I will let you guys know. I wouldn't think of handling this without you six.

And I've told them to focus on the neighborhoods surrounding the Quarter since that is where Marie's power is centered. We will work out from there in a spiral pattern, but I figure it was smarter to begin where the focus of her magic is located."

"Makes sense to me. Just let us know which streets we have," I replied as I added the fennel and stirred my mixture.

Dre tilted her head to the side. "Can we go in pairs? I'm not comfortable enough to do this on my own."

Kota shook her head from side to side rapidly as she waved one of the vials of her potion through the air. "I'm not either. No freaking way am I going out there alone. I'd be like an eight-course dinner for Marie's wendigos. No, thank you."

I laughed at Kota's choice of words. It really was too bad that Kota's magic couldn't find Lucinda for us. Smoke billowing from Dea's cauldron caught my attention and burned my eyes.

To everyone's shock Dea stood up and walked out of the house. I raced alongside Lia to the front door and watched as Dea marched across the yard. She had a scowl on her face, and her hands were clenched into fists at her sides.

Noah and Lucas joined us at the same time Kaitlyn, Dre, and Kota came out of the house. Smoke billowed out the door behind us. We all seemed to be stunned silent, and frozen in place.

I cried out when Dea spit on the pixie mound when she passed it. To add more horror to the mix, she tossed fire at the grass-covered hill. I was aghast as I watched my sister take off and leave the pixies to die.

Kaitlyn reacted before the rest of us managed to blink. The head witch put the flames out at the same time the tiny flying Fae burst from the back of the mound. They were all coughing and pale as they dropped to the ground.

I didn't bother following Dea. I needed to make sure she hadn't hurt the pixies. "Is everyone alright, Talewen?"

The pixie I thought of as the queen of the mound, ran a hand over her face. It was smeared with soot, and she was breathing too fast. "We all made it out. What happened? Are we under attack?"

I looked at Lia, then Dre and Kota. Lia went to her knees next to me and ran a hand over Talewen's blue hair. "No one is attacking. We aren't sure what happened. Deandra set the mound on fire. Something has been off with her, but I don't know what. I had assumed it was fatigue from working nights at the hospital, but now..."

"Now, we don't think that's the case," I said, picking up when Lia's words trailed off. "The Deandra we love and know would never hurt a fly, let alone a mound of pixies who she adores. I've sensed something off about her, as well."

Talewen's eyes went wide, and she moved away from Lia's touch. "She tried to kill us. If Kaitlyn hadn't acted as fast as she did, we never could have made it to the babies in the back tunnels even though I was racing there before the fire started."

They had babies? A knot formed in my chest at the thought they could have been hurt. "We would never hurt you. I want you to know that. This isn't normal for Dea, and we will find out what happened. What made you head to the babies before the fire?"

Talewen's wings fluttered rapidly behind her back, then settled after her gaze traveled around to all of us. "I felt the death magic. I was heading out of the mound and had just noted it was coming from Dea when I turned to head for the babies. The flames, heat, and smoke followed a second later."

Dre sucked in a rapid breath. "Why didn't we feel the death magic?"

Kaitlyn waved her hand from side to side. "It's difficult to detect unless you cast a spell to reveal it. Even if you had, you likely would have dismissed it as her necromantic abilities."

As long as I could recall Dea was able to see ghosts. Even when she was a little girl. I wouldn't have thought anything of it. "What the hell happened? Is she becoming dark because of her power?"

Kaitlyn shook her head. "No. Necromancers aren't bad just because they deal with the dead. Same with your sister. This is something else."

Phi lifted a shaking hand to her chest where she pressed it over her heart. "Do you think Dea was infected by the loa during the séance for the twins? She banished Baron Samedi when she did that."

Kaitlyn's eyebrow shot to her hairline. "I'm going to need more information than that. A séance wouldn't cause Dea to become possessed. She'd need to be weakened before a god could claim a foothold."

My heart lurched. "Lia is right. She's been exhausted from working doubles at the hospital. I can tell you how much that drains you. I guarantee she was diminished by that. Add the stress she felt being hounded by Giselle's spirit and she was ripe for the plucking."

Lia explained to Kaitlyn about the séance Deandra did along with the spells she cast and what happened. She added the incident she experienced during her date with Lucas near the church in the Quarter.

Kaitlyn sighed and ran a hand through her black hair. "There is no spell that Dea could cast that would give Samedi permission to inhabit her. It's more likely that when she banished him from Georgette he attached to her for the reasons you outlined, Dani. If that is what happened, we need to find Dea and help her before she is fully possessed."

I chewed on my lower lip and then let it go. "What happens if Samedi takes her over?"

Kaitlyn's face drained of color. "The god will have free rein to wreak havoc in our realm. He will be able to use his powers through Deandra to take lives and souls when he wants."

Dre crossed her arms over her chest. "How can we be sure she isn't already fully possessed?"

Kaitlyn pursed her lips. "We can't unless we cast a reveal spell. We'd better scry for Dea's location."

Lia ran to the house to grab the toothbrush Dea left at Willowberry while the rest of us prepared the items Kaitlyn would need to scry for Dea's location. Noah wrapped an arm around me as we watched. "Don't worry, Sunshine. Kaitlyn will find her."

I nodded and laid my head on his chest. I seriously loved my new magical life while also hating it at the moment. My sister's life was on the line, and I couldn't think around the worry. We had to find her before we lost her completely. I couldn't think about the alternative.

CHAPTER 18

DAHLIA

Kaitlyn sat cross-legged in the middle of the magical kitchen. The pixies had joined us. I was relieved to see they weren't holding a grudge and informing us they were leaving the plantation.

The more supernaturals we brought to the property, the more like home it felt. I worried we would lose our lives when our magical DNA was unlocked. To my surprise and pleasure, we gained more family. The pixies had become part of us, as much as Camilla.

Kaitlyn sat on the floor in front of the bowl as the water clouded over and an image of Dea walking inside a rundown building filled the space. Before I could catch an address or the specs of color amongst the fading, gray-weathered walls, the water exploded like it was Old Faithful in Yosemite National Park.

Kaitlyn cried out when the droplets hit her skin. Her flesh bubbled and looked like it was scalded by hot water. I pushed out of Lucas's arms and rushed to the head witch's side. Dani and Dre were there, already examining the wounds.

Dani looked at me over her shoulder. "Grab the first aid kit under the sink."

I turned to get it but Lucas had beat me to it. I placed a quick kiss to his lips as I took the big red box and handed it to my sister. Dani and Dre cleaned and dressed Kaitlyn's arm.

Dre taped the end of the gauze. "You should probably sit this one out and go see Kip to be healed."

Kaitlyn shook her head rapidly. "There is no way I am leaving this to you five. We are in uncharted waters here, and you guys don't know enough to go with the flow. It's best if we are all there."

I stepped back and leaned into Lucas when he wrapped an arm around my waist. It was nice to have support at a time like this. My mind was racing through a thousand different thoughts and worries without a single answer. "Does anyone know where she's at? That house could have been anywhere if you ask me."

Dani tilted her head from side to side. "There wasn't much to go by. It looked like it was one swift wind from blowing down completely, so it has to be in a depressed area with a lot of forgotten buildings."

Noah gave Dani a sympathetic look as he shook his head. "Not necessarily. It might be glamoured to look rundown. Or it might be in bad shape because it's being used for death magic, and no one is bothering to restore the structure as they go."

My forehead furrowed. "I don't understand. Why would death magic do that to a structure?"

I understood it killing the plant life nearby, but a home wasn't alive. And not all death magic killed things. When we did the soul spell here for Cami and Selene, nothing was killed in the process. And when Dea had done the séance, everything remained intact.

Lucas squeezed my side. "Death magic like Marie's uses energy from anywhere it can take it. It's usually obvious with the trees and other plants, but the houses, tombs or warehouses age much faster than would happen in nature. Because wood is a natural substance, it takes the brunt of the abuse. My gut tells me that's right outside the Quarter. The loa won't be able to stray far from the Voodoo Queen because she is sustaining him in spirit form. If Marie left her territory for long, she would risk having it taken from her. Thanks to the Twisted Sisters, the rest of the magical world is gathering the courage to take back the Quarter."

Kaitlyn stood up, wincing when her arm brushed Dre's leg in the process. "He's right. We should split up into three groups and cover the area. Look for a lot without any weeds. That's the best indicator I can think of to look for. We will see homes in desperate need of a paint job, but they'll be overrun with grass and weeds."

Lucas pressed his lips to mine as we all headed out of the house. I tried to calm my racing mind as we divided up into two cars. Lucas called Ricky and asked if he'd seen Dea, then put word out to the pack that we were looking for her. He promised we would find the house before we got downtown.

Dre nudged my shoulder. She was sitting next to me in the front seat of Lucas's truck. "Lucas's pack will find her, and we will help her."

I turned to face Kaitlyn in the backseat. "How are we going to get this thing out of her?"

Kaitlyn stopped twisting a lock of her hair around her finger. "Honestly, I'm not entirely certain. I hope an expulsion spell will do it but that's not a guarantee. The connections are stronger with witches than with mundies like Giselle and Georgette."

A vice tightened around my chest making it hard to breathe. This was the shittiest plan I'd ever been a part of, and I didn't like it one bit. The problem was that I didn't have a better solution.

I didn't pay attention as Lucas parked his truck along a street somewhere and we got out to start scouring the area. Kaitlyn came with us while Noah, Dani, and Kota went one way, and Talewen joined Phi, Dre, and Cami. The former ghoul rarely left the house, but she had come to love Dea and was as worried about her as the rest of us.

The houses all looked the same as we walked down one block and then the next. We were on what felt like our fiftieth block when Lucas's phone rang. "Tell me you've found her," he barked into the phone.

He listened and nodded then turned a smile my way making my heart leap in my chest. "Where is she?" We'd been searching for at least an hour and I was ready to lose my shit. My fingers had been sparking for the past five blocks making it difficult to hide them.

Lucas hung up the phone and pressed a quick kiss to my lips. "She's in the Treme-Lafitte neighborhood. We're only a ten-minute walk away. It's closer to head right to her rather than going back for the truck."

"Did they say if she's alright?" It was a relief to know where she was located, but I was still worried as hell. The knot in my gut had only been worse when our mom was fighting cancer. We might have seen Dea's interloper, but we were powerless to help her at the moment.

I had to run to keep up with Lucas, who had picked up his pace when he heard where she was located. A few minutes later, we turned a corner and were met with a gorgeous shifter woman. She embraced Lucas and held on a touch too long for my comfort.

I was ready to rip her face off when Lucas gently pushed her away. "You did good, Cordi. Where is she?"

Cordi pointed to a house halfway down the block. It was weathered with cracked sidewalks and was the only place with no dandelions and white clover growing all over the property.

I started running to get Dea and was stopped by Lucas's strong hands. "We need to approach with caution."

Thank God he was using his head. We could be walking right into a trap. "You're right. Let's cast a reveal spell."

Kaitlyn nodded and grabbed my hand. "Focus on the house and identify the heat signatures inside."

I took a deep breath and did as the head witch instructed, then chanted, "*Revelare,*" with Kaitlyn. The magic left me in a hot rush and settled over the house. A second later, there was one bright orange-red spot on the first floor.

"There's only one person inside," I told Lucas.

He took off, making me run to catch up with him. Kaitlyn was next to me, as was Cordi. I pounded up the three steps into the shotgun house and stopped short at what I saw.

Deandra was hunched over, drawing runes on the scarred wooden floor with her bloody finger. Her brown eyes were sunken into her head, and the circles underneath were dark purple. There were also sores all over her body. The way she was shaking made her look like a drug addict. The fact that the long, red curls of her hair were dull, faded, and snarled in a rat's nest. She was not the well-groomed Deandra I knew and loved. There was magic involved in her decline, and it scared the shit out of me.

I pulled my phone out and texted the address to the others then focused on my sister. "Dea, sweetie. I need you to stop. It's time to go home."

Dea lifted her head and snarled at me. Drool dripped from

her chin, completing her horrific look. "I'm going nowhere. I'm preparing the space before my subjects arrive with my new body. I'd take your sister's, but she's irritatingly difficult to subdue. I can't risk my last chance on her. She's deployed anchors throughout her body so I can't force her out."

There was so much to unpack in that statement. The most important was that Dea was still in there and fighting as hard as she could. That was freaking fabulous to hear. I smirked at Samedi. "You're not very smart for a god. We've foiled your plans several times over the past few months. In fact, you're in this because along with the Pleiades, we stopped Marie from taking over our soul ritual."

Dea got up and lunged at me. Lucas lowered a shoulder and knocked her down. I winced when her head bounced off the wood floorboards. She bucked and thrashed and tried to cast spells to get free.

I grabbed Kaitlyn when sparks shot from Dea's hands and singed Lucas's shirt. "Do something."

Kaitlyn shot me a dirty look. "Nothing I'm trying is working. Maybe I can coax Samedi out with some booze."

Lucas growled as Dea's foot connected with his groin. I covered myself and wanted to throw up for him. That had to hurt. He never lost his hold of her despite the pain I could see etched into the fine lines around his eyes and mouth. "Booze won't work. Whatever you're going to do, it had better be fast. We don't want Marie and her mambos showing up to cause problems."

Kaitlyn dipped her head once and wiped the sweat from her brow with the back of his arm. "I'm going to put a magical straight jacket on her so we can take her back to Willowberry."

Tears filled my eyes. My poor sister had a heart of gold and had worked so hard to get her life on track. She didn't deserve this shit. I nodded to Kaitlyn and watched Dea as she fought against Lucas.

"*Magicis recta iaccam,*" Kaitlyn chanted. Her magic shot past me like a missile, then spread out and blanketed Dea. She went still instantly, and I dropped to her side.

Lucas sat up on his knees and brushed his hair off his face. "I'm going to get the car. Noah and your sisters will be here in less than a minute, and Cordi is still outside."

I waved him off, grateful I didn't have to run all the way back there while trying to keep Dea hidden. "Go, we've got this."

Lucas was out the door a second later. I pondered our situation. "Do you think Xinar can help with this?"

Kaitlyn pursed her lips as she watched Dea. "I'm not sure. It's worth a try."

Dea muttered something in a foreign language. I felt the death leave her and grabbed hold of Kaitlyn, pulling her out of the path of Dea's spell. She needed to be gagged, as well. "*Opstruo,*" I shouted when Kaitlyn landed on top of me.

Kaitlyn sagged with relief and rolled off of me. We lay next to each other, panting on the filthy ground for several seconds until Dakota and Dani walked into the room. Dani reached down and helped me up. "What happened to her? She looks strung out."

Dakota helped Kaitlyn to her feet while I braced myself on my knees to catch my breath. "Dea's been fighting against the loa, and it's taking a lot out of her. Kaitlyn magically bound her, and I gagged her when she tried to kill her with a spell. Can you call Xinar and ask him to meet us at Willowberry? We need to find a way to free Dea."

Dani nodded and pulled her phone from her pocket. She typed in a message before checking out the runes. She snarled and pulled a vial of the potion from her pocket, then tossed it on the ground and chanted the cleansing spell. The room filled with the smell of fresh herbs before it soured into something that had bile working up my throat.

Noah lifted Dea into his arms and carried her to the truck. I sat in the back with Dre and Kota and had Noah lay Dea across our laps. Kaitlyn got in the front while the others went to get Dani's car.

Lucas sped through town and up the highway to Willow-berry. I brushed the hair from Dea's forehead. My heart cracked when I saw the hatred in her eyes. "Do you think she can hear us?"

"I'd like to believe she can. Like those that are in comas," Dre replied.

My heart constricted as I watched Dea scowl and spit at us. She couldn't move or say anything otherwise. The hand-some Asian UIS agent was leaning against a black sports car when we arrived.

Xinar's eyes widened when Lucas lifted Dea off of our laps. "Boy, you weren't kidding when you said she was possessed. I can feel death rolling off of her."

I followed behind Lucas with my keys in my hand. He took the path to the front door, given it was closer to the parlors where we would put Dea. "Can you help Kaitlyn evict this asshole?" We needed to ensure he couldn't find a foothold in anyone else.

Xinar cocked his head to the side and considered my question as I unlocked the door. "If we work together, I think it's possible."

Lucas set Dea down in one of our armchairs, and I resisted the urge to go to her side. It hurt to feel the sick-ening energy rolling off of her.

"I want everyone to cast protective barriers around them-selves before we start. I'll do one around Xinar and myself. Lia, you can do Lucas, too, can't you?" Kaitlyn's suggestion was one step behind me.

I smiled. "I was just thinking the same thing. I've got Lucas."

Kaitlyn nodded. "I figured as much. Cast your spells so we can free Deandra. We will work on developing automatic barriers that go up when you're fatigued to avoid this from happening again."

That sounded like a plan. I imagined it was a pretty advanced spell, but something we definitely needed to spend time learning. I cast the *protego* spell around Lucas and me, watching as Kaitlyn covered herself and Xinar. They stood on the side of the chair and clasped hands in front of and behind Deandra. Kaitlyn chanted the spell to purge Samedi while Xinar said something in Ancient Greek.

The air around us thickened and crackled with energy. It swirled and built around Dea. Black lightning struck my sister's body in a hundred different places at the same time. Her back arched, and tears slid from her eyes.

I cried out along with Dre and Kota. The others weren't home to see her suffer through this, thankfully. Lucas went to wrap his arms around me, but I had already grabbed Dre's arm, and she had grabbed Kota's. Lucas put his hands on my shoulders, letting me know he was there for me.

I watched as sweat poured from Kaitlyn's face and the blood vessels rose to the surface of Xinar's face and arms. The front door opened, and I immediately drew upon power from Dre and Kota then shouted a protection spell over Phi, Dani, Cami, and Noah.

Not a second after I finished that spell Deandra's mouth opened, and her head flew back. Black smoke poured from her mouth and coalesced into the loa; Baron Samedi next to her. His skeletal features and the elaborate top hat made my stomach roil. He gave us an evil smile, tipped his hat, and vanished from the room. I turned in a circle, searching to make sure he didn't reappear somewhere else. I felt something push against my awareness, and each of my sister's gasped at the same time I did.

Kaitlyn sagged against the chair. "Your wards forced him out. Without Dea as a host, his malevolent intentions weren't permitted on the property."

"Thank God!" I exclaimed.

Dea's head dropped as she collapsed against the chair cushion, and the tendons on the side of her neck flattened. She was covered in sweat and panting, as she smiled at us. "Thank you guys! It's a relief to be alone in my body again. I tried to tell you a hundred times, but Samedi always managed to tie my tongue."

I wrapped an arm around her. "How much do you remember?"

Dea sighed and rubbed a hand down her face. "I remember everything. It was like living in a haze when he surged forward and took over. Other times he was in the background as a silent threat. Marie visited me and said if I could make the house useful, she would give me untold riches. As if that was enough. He couldn't force me until I was weaker from constantly fighting him."

Kaitlyn smiled at Dea. "You were very brave. We need to stop the mambo and Marie. Samedi admitted this was his last chance. You didn't happen to hear anything, did you?"

Dea nodded. "I overheard Marie tell a mambo named Rachelle that they would use her house if I failed to prepare the house I was working on."

I released Dea. "Then we need to find Rachelle's house. Right now, though, we need to get you some food. And a shower. You smell like a sewer."

Dani lifted a hand. "I've already asked Kip to stop by and heal those wounds. We don't want them getting infected."

Dea smacked my arm. "They're the reason I smell so bad. I was sweating like a pig while trying to stop him from hurting me. He needed to use my blood, and every cut he made, I stopped the flow before he got more than one symbol drawn."

I went over, in my mind, how my sister had been over the past week so that I would know if anything like this happened again. Forewarned was forearmed. Hopefully, I'd learned enough to take action immediately if it should happen again.

It could have been so much worse if we hadn't located her in time. I shuddered to think what shape she would have been in if Marie made Dea slit the victim's throat to complete the process for Samedi's possession. Deandra would never have been able to live with herself. It was difficult to remind myself that we'd averted the crisis and everything was alright.

CHAPTER 19

DANIELLE

*F*ocusing on the second line parade was difficult to do when I knew Kaitlyn was trying to locate Rachelle as we prepared the celebration of Ava's mother's life. The Six Twisted Sisters had never failed a client, and I wouldn't let these magical disasters interfere now. We weren't paid for handling the cases, so we needed to keep growing our business.

I adjusted the sash over Ava's shoulder. "There you go. That's perfect. And just in time. The conductor is ready to go."

Ava's eyes filled with tears. "Thank you all so much. I couldn't have done a better job honoring my mother. She would have loved every detail you put into this."

I smiled and gave Ava a hug, then checked to make sure Dre and Kota were done helping Ava's aunts and uncles with their parasols or sashes. "We will be at the back if you need anything."

Ava nodded then held her mother's picture up and started marching down the street. The band started playing, and before my sisters and I made it to the tail end of the parade everyone was dancing to the jazzy tune.

Lia and Kota held up beaded necklaces and encouraged bystanders to join the celebration. That was part of the fun in the second line parades. Tourists always joined the fun. The fleur de lis, beads, feathers, and jazz band drew them like flies to honey. I had to admit I loved it because it was the perfect representation of the city where I was born.

It made my blood sing. It was all the more special because I helped make this happen for Ava and her family. Their smiles and the way they danced spoke to the fun they were having in Olivia's honor.

I wished Dea could have been here to tell us if Olivia was with us as we followed the band down the street. Phi was home with Dea, making sure she got the rest she needed after her ordeal with Samedi. It was nice to throw my hands in the air and dance along with everyone else. Lia, Dre, and Kota were right there with me. The parade was blissfully mundane and something that connected me to my mundie life. For several minutes I wasn't a witch. I was nothing more than a woman that had started a business with her sisters.

We were half a block from Lafitte's Bar when my magical life collided with my mundane one. A woman sauntered from a dark alley and joined our procession. When she turned her head and smiled back at me, my blood froze in my veins.

A skeletal face overlayed hers, making her smile and blue eyes blur out of focus. I would never forget that face or the top hat. Samedi was still freaking here. I grabbed Lia's hand and pointed to the woman.

We'd reached the bar, and the woman was heading for Lucas, who was sitting at a group of tables. We'd sent him and Noah to hold the tables for Ava and her family. Lia gasped and ran for Lucas.

"God bless it," Dre muttered.

"How the fuck do we get rid of that god?" Kota snarled a second later.

We all hurried forward and were stopped when tiny red demons jumped from the rafters and ran so fast that they blurred. I spun in a circle, almost falling over in my haste to find the newcomer and follow Samedi.

Xinar raced around the corner, slamming into me. He caught me before I fell on my ass. "Where did they go?"

I steadied myself and shook my head. "I have no idea. They moved too fast to follow, but we have a bigger problem. Samedi is here."

Xinar scanned the bar. "Your sister has her shifter protected, but we need to get rid of that god."

I clenched my jaw. "How do you propose we do that?"

"I can try and cast a spell we were taught in training." Xinar shrugged one shoulder. "It's meant for Greek gods and goddesses, so it might not work on the loa."

Dre rolled her eyes. "We don't give a shit. Give it a go."

Xinar inclined his head and brushed his hands down the front of his suit jacket. "Get ready for hurricane force winds." With that warning, Xinar said something in Ancient Greek. I didn't know the language but imagined it was something along the lines of banishing all godly powers from the area.

Nothing happened for several seconds after he cast his spell. That all changed the second Ava lifted her drink to toast her mother. The wind started blowing through the area, sending tourists screaming and running for cover.

Chairs that weren't bolted down were picked up and carried down the street toward us. The woman that was possessed clutched her throat and started choking. Lucas sprang from the table and then shoved Lia behind his body.

Lightning crackled in the air around us, making the mundies scream. The bolts of electricity traveled to the entity as it separated from the woman. Lucas caught her before she collapsed and then set her in a chair.

Xinar ducked when the bolts of electricity coalesced into a person-sized funnel cloud. It burst apart a second later, and the wind stopped. The mundies stood up and came out of the various businesses talking about the odd weather.

Ava ordered a round of drinks to replace the ones that had been ruined, and in true NOLA fashion, she continued the celebration for her mom. Those that lived here were used to dealing with weather catastrophes without letting it stop them from living.

I accepted a drink from Ava and watched as Xinar moved to the back of the bar. My sisters joined me and we watched the celebration, making sure Ava and her family had everything they needed.

As soon as the mundies dispersed, I approached Xinar and asked him what was bothering him. His energy had set Noah and Lucas on edge, making them prowl around the block more than once during the time we were there.

"Don't you feel the difference?" Xinar asked.

My sisters and I shared a look, and I focused on my magic. "It feels different down here, but I can't say why."

Dahlia lifted a hand. "I felt it shift when you used your Underworld powers."

"It did. I have no idea why but I'm worried my banishment upset the balance in the area," Xinar admitted.

My eyes flew wide, and my heart started hammering in my chest. Noah wrapped his arms around me from behind. "We can't worry about that right now. We need to prepare to stop the mambos. Kaitlyn found Rachelle and will meet us at her house in an hour."

I wanted to sink into Noah's warmth, but I couldn't. We

had too much shit to deal with. He was right. We had no idea if this change in the balance was a good or a bad thing. For all I knew, it would favor the good paranormals living there.

"I need to change out of this shirt and these shoes, then. I can't fight in two-inch, heeled boots," I replied. It was incredibly embarrassing that I could barely walk in them.

Noah pressed a kiss to my neck. "I brought the potion, your tennis shoes, and a t-shirt."

I stepped out of his embrace and lifted one eyebrow at him. "Did you know she would locate Rachelle?"

He twined his fingers with mine and led me down the street to our car. "No, but I've learned it's always better to be prepared."

He wasn't wrong about that. It hadn't been long since being prepared meant packing snacks, changes of clothes, and water wherever I went. When you had children, you needed to be ready for just about anything.

CHAPTER 20

DANIELLE

I felt like a common criminal as we crouched in some shrubs two houses down from Rachelle's house. We'd gotten lucky when Dea overheard Marie mention the name of the mambo's house they would use for the ritual. Otherwise, there wasn't a chance we would have discovered the location in time.

Given the activity in and around the house, the ritual was happening shortly. We were waiting for more shifters to arrive so they could tackle the mambos before they entered the house. There were half a dozen members of the coven around the area and all were armed with the cleansing spell.

They knew one of their own was at risk and had been more than eager to stop this ritual. It was nice to be so prepared for a battle rather than how we'd been ambushed in the past.

Don't get too cocky. That's when shit always goes sideways. Knowing that was true didn't change how I viewed the situation. Having Kaitlyn, Noah, Lucas, and the various shifters and witches at our side was a far cry better than when Lia and I faced off with the skinwalker while Noah and Lucas were occupied nearby.

It felt like we were settling into this new magical life rather well, even with the unexpected paranormal detective work. The party planning side of the business was doing better than I could ever have expected when we purchased the plantation.

None of us were rolling in money, but we were able to pay the bills on the place and feed ourselves without worry. Lia and I had been prepared to eat Top Ramen, if need be. Regular meals were a huge bonus.

I could honestly say that I was enjoying the cases that were thrown our way. Initially, I had fought against dealing with them. Since accepting them as part of our lives, I was able to appreciate how they brought us even closer as sisters. Now that we were utilizing our powerful allies, I was actually enjoying the chaos of running around trying to put the puzzle pieces together and make sense of them to avert total disasters.

"It's time, Sunshine. Are you ready?" Noah's deep voice made me shiver at the same time, it snagged my attention.

I held up my vial of potion. "Yes, sir. I'm ready to roll. Has anyone seen Leveau?"

Noah shook his head as he crept toward Rachelle's house. I followed behind, careful to keep us cloaked. Kaitlyn warned the mambos would sense our spells at work. Our hope was that with so many of us approaching at the same time, it would confuse them.

When we made it to the edge of Rachelle's lawn without incident, I almost whooped with joy. We were going to make it inside without being stopped. The shifters and witches could deal with the mambos that were outside.

A second later, fate decided to prove Kaitlyn's point to me as a dead mastiff popped up through the dirt in front of me. I'd kept my eyes on the voodoo priestesses and their actions, forgetting they could animate the dead.

The dog's fur was mottled with worms and beetles dropping from missing chunks of flesh like rice. I nearly passed out from the smell of roadkill when it snarled at me and went for my throat. Noah knocked me out of the way and kicked the dog's head from its body. The ground rumbled all around us before it rippled like a wave coming to shore. Small animals of all kinds popped their half-decomposed bodies through the soil.

A shudder of revulsion traveled through me as I decided to run for the backdoor like planned and leave the dead things to the others. We'd lost our element of surprise and needed to make sure we weren't locked out of the house.

The door opened before I reached it, and Kaitlyn raced into the kitchen beside me. "We need to find the basement. That's most likely the location for the ritual space Lia saw in her vision."

I turned to start my search and ran into a young woman with long curly black hair, dark brown skin, and a scowl that could peel paint from the walls. "I thought I smelled a witch in the house. Thank you for coming. We couldn't have had the proper gifts for Samedi without you. We had hoped we'd get a few more inside before activating the barrier."

I spun around, and Lucinda was there holding a wicked-looking, curved knife that was bigger than my arm. She wagged her finger in my face. "Ah, ah. You're not going anywhere."

Lucinda and the other mambo chanted something in what sounded like Creole, but I couldn't be sure because I was busy trying to focus enough to call my fire. Before I opened my fist, fire exploded outside. Noah cried out when he flew back from the back door.

I caught sight of his blackened fingers as he soared away from the house. There was death magic on the house. I met Kaitlyn's gaze, and she mouthed a spell to me. I focused on exactly what she told me, inviting in life.

"*Inverso*," I shouted a second after Kaitlyn. White light burst from my chest, leaving me breathless.

Spots danced in my vision, and my head swam. I reached for Kaitlyn when my legs gave out. I missed and crashed into a wall that held me up. An arm wrapped around my waist, and one of the mambos dragged me to a door then down a set of stairs.

A tight grip on my arm kept me from tumbling down the wooden steps. I tried to fight against the mambo, but it was useless. My magic had rebounded on me, zapping me of every ounce of energy I had.

The world darkened around me, and I was thrown onto a cold, stone floor before I knew what was happening. My knee impacted the hard surface first. That was going to hurt later. I pushed to a sitting position and tried to focus on my surroundings.

Someone landed on top of me, forcing me back to the ground again. "What?' Kaitlyn sounded drunk as she struggled to finish her question. I finally managed to shove her off of me.

Glass clinked when I used my hands to shove my upper body off the ground. The potion. I still had it in my hand. Knowing that I needed to cast a spell with it, I held off on using it. There was no way I could cast anything at the moment.

My eyes cleared enough that I could see the stone table in front of us. A grunt followed by a woman screaming Kaitlyn's name snapped me to attention. My head still swam enough that I didn't trust myself, but I was able to take in our surroundings.

There was a woman dressed in a loose black dress with her hands tied behind her back. Lucinda had her long fingers wrapped around one of the woman's biceps. Tears streamed down her face as the mambo forced her onto the table.

"Brianna," Kaitlyn called out.

We needed help. There was another mambo, this one far more powerful, hidden in the shadows around us. My current position kept me from getting a good view of what was to the left of us.

I focused my energy on the death magic I felt outside. Wanting to cancel out the spell by bombarding the area with life, I dialed in my thoughts and intent, then chanted the spell under my breath. I sent the energy to the zombie animals and fire.

Kaitlyn frowned at me before she followed suit. Thankfully, Lucinda and the other mambo were too busy tying Brianna to the altar to notice what we were doing. My gaze was trained on the window above our heads, so I saw when the fire went out.

Xinar, Noah, and Lucas jumped down the stairs without setting one foot on them less than five seconds later. Lucinda cried out, "Rachelle, do it now!" Then thrust the hand holding the weapon at the young mambo.

Rachelle took the weapon and lifted it over Brianna's body. Noah leaped over the stone table and knocked Rachelle to the ground while Lucas used the claws at the ends of his fingers to slice through the ropes holding Brianna.

I pushed to my feet and limped over to help Brianna off the table while Kaitlyn and Lucas focused on the shadows. The spirit of Baron Samedi barreled toward Lucas. Time seemed to stand still as the loa headed right for Lucas's chest.

Samedi bounced off of an invisible barrier before ever touching Lucas.

"Stay the hell away from my boyfriend," Lia snarled from the top of the stairs.

I wanted to cry with relief, but I needed to help stop the ceremony. Lifting my arm into the air, I slammed the vial to the ground, making the bright green potion spill all over the floor. The spell left my mouth before I lost my concentration.

In an instant, my magic collided with the voodoo spells and exploded. The smell of bleach and dead rodents filled the space, along with black smoke. My lungs seized, making me cough while my eyes watered, making it impossible to see.

I heard glass breaking before a cool breeze blew through the room, carrying the stench and smoke with it. Whoever was in the shadows shrieked and vanished in a flash of bright red light.

When it all cleared, we were left facing Samedi who was looking at me. His look made me recall the feeling of something hooking inside me days ago. I'd ignored it because I hadn't felt anything else, but I knew he was tied to me. He was still in the basement because I was holding him in our plane.

I'd put up a barrier before coming here, and it was still in place. It had saved me from the worst of the death magic and was the reason I was still alive. Wanting that small tether to the loa gone, I focused on prying it loose, then whispered, "*Ut ex.*"

Samedi bared his teeth at me and reversed course to head to me. My hand went into the air, and I called the air to keep him away from me. Brianna shook at my side, then grabbed my arm. "We need to cleanse the air, as well. It will force the loa to leave. His time on Earth is up, and without a tether here, he will return to his realm."

Xinar met my gaze and nodded. I searched for Lia and Kaitlyn. They were in the shadows where the entity had vanished. "Help us banish this asshole."

My sister and the head witch left the shadows and joined hands with me and Brianna while Lucas and Noah handled the two mambos. I tuned out what they did to the voodoo practitioners and focused on banishing Samedi. When Kaitlyn nodded, we all shouted the same banishment spell together.

Xinar's voice joined in our chant. His words were different, but his magic complemented ours and joined it. The two different powers twined together and pushed against the loa. Samedi snarled, fighting us. I redoubled my efforts and poured more energy into my casting.

Baron Samedi glared in my direction. "This isn't over. I'll be back and next time I will make sure the Twisted Sisters can't stand in my way."

After he left us with that threat, the loa disappeared in a flash of purple light. The smell of cloves lingered in the loa's wake. My heart slowed when I realized the evil voodoo god was finally gone. Part of me thought this had been too easy. It left a niggle of doubt that Samedi was actually gone.

Xinar lifted his hands in the air. "I can't sense any lingering energy from the loa. We need to be alert. There is a chance he still has a hold on your plane. Until we know for sure, keep your guard up at all times."

Lucinda and Rachelle remained slumped in the corner. Kaitlyn had already informed the paranormal police officer for the Southern region of the United States that they needed to be taken to their prison. The existence of Coldwater Correctional center was another issue I'd set aside to learn more about later.

I didn't understand the frantic desire to be here. "Why the hell do they want to cross to Earth so bad? They're gods in their realm. I'd think they'd want to be where they are most powerful." I rubbed my sore knee, hoping I hadn't cracked my kneecap.

Xinar brushed the blood from his suit jacket. "Like demons, being here allows them to experience power and pleasures in the flesh. It's not the same for gods in their realm. They gain something from being here, but their presence upsets the balance. Many gods have weakened significantly over the centuries as mundies forget their importance and they are worshipped less and less, so another reason they want to come here is to obtain more power. They cannot steal magic from the other side. Not to mention the renewed belief when they are seen, it boosts their standing."

My stomach revolted as I considered what Xinar had said. It was a good thing that gods couldn't just pop onto our plane of existence or we would be overrun by greedy beings taking our power and leaving destruction in their wake.

CHAPTER 21

DAHLIA

"**C**lose your eyes," Dani told me as she brandished a makeup brush in her hand.

She'd already styled my hair while Phi and Dea helped Dre and Kota. Tonight was the Roaring Twenties cocktail party for Albar and his office. My hair was in perfect finger waves, and she was now creating a smoky eye for me.

"Is the caterer here yet?" I asked as I went through a mental list of what we needed to do before guests arrived in a few minutes.

"They're in the prep kitchen and ready to serve when I tell them," Phi replied from my right.

"Brezok and the band are both set up in the men's parlor," Dre added.

Dani swept the brush over my eyelid several times. "And done. You look outstanding, Lia."

I rolled my eyes. "You didn't use that much makeup. I can't believe how fast we got this one together. You are nothing short of the best, Dani. And why didn't I get a dress that looks that good on me?"

Dani was wearing a cream-colored dress and feathered headband. The top was made of lace over a silk slip, and the cap sleeves covered her shoulders but didn't extend down her upper arms.

Dani twisted back and forth, making the knee-length skirt flare around her. "I look like a potato."

Kota snorted. "You do not. I, however, look like a green apple in this dress."

Dakota had a full figure and didn't see how pretty she was most of the time. I understood she was uncomfortable in the getup. I wasn't exactly relaxed in the silver sequined flapper-style dress.

Deandra lifted one hand into the air and held the other down by her side. "We all look fabulous, and we are going to rock this party!"

Malik poked his head in the door. "Albar is here."

We'd enlisted the guys tonight because we weren't sure how many servers we would need. The caterer brought the food but not the waiters or waitresses. Albar agreed to the men in our lives walking around with trays while we made sure nothing else was needed.

Phi finished the last touches on Dre, then we left the women's parlor where we'd gotten ready. Cami was already at the bottom of the stairs, standing next to the black and gold balloon arch Dani and Dea had set up around the back-drop. I'd painted some plywood black, then glued a geometric design I'd cut out with the laser and painted gold.

Albar's gaze shifted from the house to us. "This place is beyond everything I expected. How did you make that photo booth? It's not one of those plastic sheets like most places use."

I smiled, glad that he appreciated the effort we had taken.

Dre and I barely finished the thing an hour before. "That's part of the Twisted Sisters magic."

One of Albar's eyebrows rose. "You used magic?"

Dre held up her red fingertips. "Not at all. We have a laser engraver that allows us to create custom wood, glass, and plastic items for events. Few locations can offer what we can."

Dani gestured to the bookcases on his right. "Would you like to see the parlor where your event will be held before your guests arrive?"

Albar's smile grew when he saw the bookcases. He clapped his hands together and laughed. "You did it! I can't believe you got all this done and stopped Marie's mambo from bringing back Baron Samedi."

Dani pulled on the furthest bookcase and slid both of them to the side, opening the space Kota, Dani, Phi, and Dea had overhauled while Dre and I built the backdrop. Gold and black decorations dominated the area. The bar height tables had gold lamè tablecloths with black wine bottles filled with white feathers. Strands of what looked like pearls wound around the vases and there were eight-foot-tall columns of gold and black balloons throughout the room.

Albar went straight for the five-foot tall image of the woman in the black and gold dress hanging on the wall next to the bar where Brezok was dressed in a tuxedo and in his human form.

"This looks exactly like the picture you showed me. I can't believe you used that as inspiration and managed all of this. As soon as this is done, we should talk about next quarter's theme," Albar said.

Dani inclined her head. "We look forward to it."

Cami stuck her head inside the parlor. "The guests are arriving. Would you like to greet them, or shall I send them in?"

Albar moved forward with the biggest smile on his face. "I'd like to do that if you don't mind. I want to see their faces."

We all filed out of the room. Albar went to the front doors while my sisters and I ducked back inside the women's parlor to watch. The gargoyle left the front doors open as he greeted his co-workers and then instructed them to find their way inside the speakeasy through the bookcases.

The entryway was filled with people dressed up to fit the theme. And they all seemed to want to go through the bookcases one at a time, so we heard everything they thought about what they'd seen so far. I couldn't help the smile that spread across my face when his guests talked about how much they loved the setup. We'd done a great job for such short notice.

I almost panicked when one couple paused in the photo booth area and grabbed some of the fun props we had laid out on the table. Camilla was quick to offer to take their picture for them. It felt right to have her out there front and center.

Lucas and the rest of the husbands joined us in the parlor to let us know the food was ready. Dani told them to start offering food to the guests. It was a good call, given that they were already drinking.

Brezok practically glowed as people hovered around the bar. We left the parlor when the music started playing and snuck past some of the guests. I hovered near the exit, so I could help Cami at the photo booth if needed.

It wasn't long before Albar abandoned his post at the door. He left one of the bookcases open for any stragglers. He was the life of the party as he milled around the room.

Movement in the entryway made me turn to see who had just arrived. My feet carried me out of the room in an instant. Cami slammed the bookcase shut and looked at me with panic written across her face.

Imps were pouring into the house from the front doors. There were at least two dozen of the tiny devils. This time not all of them were completely red. Some had black horns with a black spade at the end of their tail, as well.

I scrambled to think about what to do and managed to mutter a spell to freeze them by the time Dani and Dre joined us. Dani's face went pale as she stumbled toward me. "How the hell did they cross the wards?"

"They mean you no harm," Xinar answered from the doorway. "They're likely here to feed off of the revelry. Parties are chaotic by nature and appeal to imps."

Albar came out of the parlor, and his mouth dropped open. There were tiny demons hanging from our crystal chandelier, the bookcases, and the railing going up the twin staircases. "This can't be happening. If my co-workers see this, shit is going to hit the fan."

Xinar waved a hand through the air. "The sisters are prepared for everything and called me to deal with this." Like in the alley, Xinar chanted something in a foreign language, making the imps disappear.

Albar sighed in relief. "You guys are good. I was worried there for a minute. I came to let you know Brezok needs more champagne."

I smiled and gestured for him to return to his guests. "We will deliver the next case right away."

Dreya was already moving down the hall to the kitchen that we used inside the main house. It was where we were chilling the champagne and storing the other alcohol. I shook my head, grateful Aidon had sent this UIS agent to the area. That could have turned into a disaster.

"Please tell me you're sticking around, NOLA. I have a feeling we are going to need you," I told Xinar.

"I have been stationed here for now." Xinar took the box of champagne from Dre and carried it to the bookcases.

Dani opened the panel for him. "I hope your assignment never changes. We're going to need your help with how we can keep the demons out. We can't have imps crashing our parties."

Xinar inclined his head. "That's smart given the number of them I have sensed in the area. I've been working non-stop to send them home."

That news barely evoked a reaction in me. Imps were nothing compared to the shit we'd already dealt with. My mind brought his comment from the other day, after the second line parade, to the front of my mind. Perhaps this was an indication that he was indeed right about the balance in New Orleans being off.

Either way, it wasn't something we were going to stop this party to handle. My mind was churning through ideas on how to deal with what we might be facing, but that was something for another day. Right now, I needed a drink and a canape.

DOWNLOAD the next book in the Twisted Sisters Midlife Maelstrom series, French Quarter Fae HERE! Then turn the page for a preview.

EXCERPT FROM FRENCH QUARTER FAE BOOK #4

✒

DAHLIA

I moaned as the garlic, basil, and cheese burst over my taste buds. "That is so freaking delicious. I need the recipe for this pizza dough. Mine always tastes more like bread. It needs to be chewier like this."

Lucas lifted his hand to get the attention of the waiter. "Can you bring Chef Daniels out here, please? Tell him Lucas is here to talk to him."

My mouth parted in surprise. I learned something new about Lucas every day. It was slightly disturbing to think of his commitment to me despite how little we actually knew of one another. I was adjusting to the magical world rapidly, but my mind still operated like a mundie in some fundamental ways.

Cocking my head to the side, I smirked at him. "Do you know people everywhere? I thought this was a mundie-owned business."

Lucas set his piece of pizza down and wiped his mouth. "I've been alive longer than you, Flower."

The reminder of our age differences used to make me uncomfortable. I was in my mid-forties while he was in his mid-seventies. For mundies, that would have been a major difference. Lucas was a shifter and they lived long lives and aged at a slower rate than humans. No one knew how my sisters and I would age from here because we were magical mutts.

A few short months ago, we were normal mundies that had purchased a rundown plantation together. We changed completely when a powerful witch visited us at Willowberry and lifted a curse on our property, unlocking our dormant magical DNA in the process.

"You don't have to try and impress me with your connections. Having your pack help me fight zombies did that." I smiled at him as I took another bite.

A handsome guy with close-cropped, brown hair approached our table right then. He clapped Lucas's extended hand. "Hey, Luc. How's it going?"

"It's great, Nigel. I'd like to introduce my mate, Dahlia. She and her five sisters own the Willowberry Plantation." Lucas gestured to me as I tried my best to chew fast and swallow my food.

My cheeks heated as I dipped my head and forced the cheesy dough down my gullet. It got stuck, making me choke and start coughing. Lucas handed me my water and patted my back, asking if I was alright. It took a couple of seconds before I managed to get the wad down past my esophagus so I could breathe and speak again.

Nodding, I shook the hand Nigel had been holding out to me. "Sorry. That went down the wrong pipe."

Nigel smiled, revealing even white teeth. "It's alright. Luc caught you mid-bite. I've heard of the fabulous events you and your sisters throw. How did this riffraff land such a gem as yourself?"

I chuckled and laid a hand over Lucas's on the table. "I'm the one that got lucky."

Lucas turned his hand over and twined our fingers together. "Fate brought us together."

"The way I hear it, she also brought the sisters into our world to turn it on its head," Nigel added.

My gaze traveled over Nigel's face, from his blue eyes to his slightly crooked nose and big smile. He was magazine-worthy but nothing told me what kind of paranormal creature he was.

Lucas leaned toward me. "He's a mage."

"Ah," I said as I looked up at Nigel. "I'm still getting used to everything in this world, so you'll have to excuse me."

Nigel tilted his head from side to side. "It's understandable. It's a major change from what you were used to, and there are so many nuances and things to consider. Although, from what I hear, you and your sisters are making your own rules."

My back straightened, and a smile swept over my face. I'd always marched to my own drummer. Especially when it meant trampling injustice. That was not something I had ever tolerated. It was one reason I went into social work to begin with. "We think of it as redefining guidelines. No one individual should have absolute power over others. Just because something has been done a certain way doesn't mean it should stay that way."

Lucas beamed with pride. "Your integrity is one reason so many are supporting your changes. They know you aren't trying to step in and take power for yourself."

"Lucas is right. What you and your sisters have stirred up has given other leaders the courage to take action on their own," Nigel added.

The thought that we sparked something by freeing the necromancers from Marie Leveau's control was thrilling. Change was good. And from what I'd seen, the magical world in New Orleans needed it. "That's encouraging. We'd hate to do all of this and have her force everyone back in line."

"I can't see that happening. Anyway, is there anything I can do for you before I go back to the kitchen?" I welcomed Nigel's change of subject. The last thing I wanted to do during my date with Lucas was get involved in a political debate.

Lucas nodded as he let go of my hand and picked up his slice. "Lia and I were just talking about how you get your dough to the perfect consistency."

My cheeks were pink, but I wasn't going to turn away any advice. "It's nice and chewy which is something I can never manage."

Nigel chuckled as he waved his hands in front of him. "You should start with using a long rise time before you knead, knead, knead it. It also helps to use a recipe with more salt, as well. Honestly, I credit the flavor and consistency of mine to the starter that I use. It's been in my family for seventy years."

A gasp escaped my mouth. "I'll try your tips, but I'm not going to count on it being different. That starter is no doubt one key to your success. My former mother-in-law used to have a sourdough starter she got from her grandmother, and it made the best bread I've ever eaten."

"If you're familiar with using a starter, I'm happy to share some of mine with you," Nigel offered. "Although, I shouldn't. It'd be bad for business." He winked at me, making Lucas scowl at his friend.

"I'll take it because my sister Dakota will be able to work wonders with it. I'm not actually familiar with using starters. I enjoy cooking but didn't have much time to perfect my skills," I admitted. There was no need to tell him I didn't inherit the starter from Leo's mom. She didn't even speak to me anymore.

Nigel inclined his head as something near the kitchen caught his eye. "I'll have some brought out to you. It was nice meeting you, Dahlia. I look forward to seeing you again."

I held up a hand. "I'd like that. In fact, I know you don't offer catering, but I would love to talk to you about doing special events at Willowberry. My brother-in-law put in a stone pizza oven when we renovated a while back."

Nigel's eyes lit up. "That's an intriguing offer. I've wanted to expand. Lucas has my number. Let's chat soon."

Lucas and I thanked the chef before he took off to the kitchen at a rapid pace. Lucas lifted my hand and kissed the back of it. "Are you ready to head home? I have more planned for you this evening."

My mind raced with naughty thoughts as I wiped my mouth and dropped my napkin on my plate. "I like the way you think, Chief."

Lucas wrinkled his nose as he signaled the waiter again. "I'm not sure I like that nickname," he told me before focusing on the server. "Can we get a couple of boxes and the check, please?"

I smiled sweetly at Lucas as the waiter left to do as asked. "You're stuck with it now. You shouldn't be such a dominating man, and I'd have come up with something else. Perhaps you'd like stud muffin better."

Lucas chuckled as he shook his head. "Chief it is, then." Lucas paid the bill and accepted the boxes and containers of dough from the server. We were out the door and down the street, headed for the parking lot where his truck was parked across the French Quarter.

My arms prickled with an unfamiliar energy. I scanned our surroundings, searching for the source of my discomfort.

Everything looked like it should. The restaurants and bars were crowded with patrons. The mundies laughed and joked with one another with drinks in their hands. The moon and stars above were bright and the heat of a summer night caused a light sheen of sweat to cover my body.

Of course, that could have been caused by one of those 'heat things' as Deandra called them. At forty years old, Dea had only experienced a couple of them, so she wasn't truly familiar with how awful hot flashes could be.

Unable to banish the sensation that something was wrong, I tugged on Lucas's hand. "Do you feel that?"

Lucas lifted the bag in his hand and gestured to a darkened courtyard in front of us. "If I'm not mistaken, there's a vampire up ahead."

I moved closer to his side when he said that as I recalled the one encounter Dani and I'd had with a couple of vamps at Brezok's bar a while back. They'd put us under a thrall with the intention of making us compliant, so they could feed from us. That was after Phoebe told us how vampires in my city had nearly killed Stella. None of that made me like them much.

I was so focused on the area where Lucas believed the vampire was hiding that I missed the monster loping across Jackson Square. Lucas shoved the bag into my hand and shifted his hands into claws at the same time, people started screaming. I opened my purse, hoping to find a weapon but came up empty. Instead, I grabbed my phone and asked Siri to text Kaitlyn about sending someone to my location to deal with mundies before they got away. I could see numerous cell phones come out with their cameras aimed at the sight of Lucas charging a creature that looked like a cross between a bear and a dog. It's orange eyes, and sharp claws had me shaking as my boyfriend rammed into the thing.

The beast tossed Lucas over its head, making him crash

into a group of mundies that were recording the showdown. These videos were going to expose the magical world and destroy countless lives, so I took a moment to concentrate on my intent on creating an electromagnetic pulse that would disable the electronics in the area. I needed to keep my new world safe.

Getting a clear picture was easy, thanks to Hollywood and the countless shows I'd seen where thieves or spies disabled alarms with a device that did something similar. With my intent clear in my mind, I chanted, *"Electro pulsum."* Energy rushed out of me as soon as the words left my mouth. The force of it made me stumble forward. My movement caught the monster's attention and it was headed right for me.

Ignoring the mundies cursing about their cell phones not working, I ran toward the park a few feet away. There were fewer mundies to get hurt there. I conjured my witch fire as I went. I considered trying to shift my hands into dragon talons but that took too much effort for me still, so I went with the easier task of my amber flames.

Claws scraped across my back, and I fell to my knees, scraping the shit out of them as I hit the sidewalk. Curses flew from my mouth as I lost the bag with the pizza dough starter and our leftovers. I was really looking forward to trying my hand at the dough with Dakota.

Lucas was there before the monster managed to get in another blow. I watched his fist slam into the side of the bear-dog's head. As a shifter and the alpha of his pack, Lucas was strong as hell, yet his punch didn't faze the beast.

Lucas wrapped an arm around the creature's neck and yanked it away from me. I called up my fire again and pressed my palms to the monster's legs. It ignited the fur that covered its limbs instantly. I willed the flames to burn through flesh and muscle but not travel and hurt Lucas. I couldn't let it go completely or Lucas would get hurt.

I kicked the monster making it drop to its knees. Lucas sliced open the side of its neck, making blood gush out of the wound. Mundies started screaming then. I imagined before that, they assumed we were filming a movie or something. New Orleans was a popular location for movie and television production. I needed to keep the mundies contained.

"Nolite movere," I blurted the second the thought entered my mind. I didn't have time to firm up my intent. My mind whirled as I watched Lucas handle the monster, wondering where it came from. It had a dark green aura with black lines running throughout. I coaxed my flames to spread over the monster when Lucas lifted his touch from the thing. The scent of burning fur and flesh turned my stomach.

"Lia," Kaitlyn cried out.

My head snapped in her direction, and I winced when the movement made the cut along my upper back pulled. "Thank God you're here. I have no idea where this thing came from. It just started attacking. I fried the phones and stopped the mundies from leaving. I didn't want to try and erase their memories of this incident. I was afraid I'd fry their brains instead." The words came out in rapid-fire when the head witch stopped in front of me.

Kaitlyn turned me gently with a hand on my shoulder. I felt heat emanate from her hand and seep into the wound. I realized she had stopped the bleeding when the warm trickle down my skin stopped. "You did well. I'm glad you didn't try to erase anyone's memories. All you would have done was turn their brains to mush. We leave that to vampires. Anton is on his way here to help deal with this mess."

I couldn't relax with her assurances, but I did bend and pick up the bag I'd dropped, hoping the dough and leftovers were still good inside. Lucas kicked the creature, and I extinguished my fire. "What is that? And why would it attack in the French Quarter?"

Kaitlyn covered her nose as she bent closer to the thing. I couldn't imagine closing the distance to that thing. It smelled bad enough from several feet away. "I didn't get a good look at it before your flames burned it. What did it look like?" Kaitlyn asked.

I recounted what I'd seen to Kaitlyn at the same time, Lucas's eyes narrowed on a guy heading in our direction from Decatur. It looked like he was coming from the river on the other side of that street.

"It sounds like a barghest. It's a Fae creature," Kaitlyn said then followed my gaze when she noticed I wasn't paying attention. The head witch lifted a hand. "Thank you for coming Anton. As you can see, we need your assistance erasing the last half an hour from the minds of the mundies that witnessed this incident."

Anton inclined his head, then settled his stormy gray eyes on me. "I'd be happy to help, but only because I assume you aren't the ones that brought this beast from the Fae realm."

Lucas snarled at the vampire. "We all have to work together to protect our identities. Your kind would be hunted first. And, no, we didn't bring it here."

Kaitlyn lifted her hands and gestured around them. "Lucas is right, we have to cooperate with each other. Anton came when I asked Lucas. He's here to help. Now, what matters is keeping the magical world a secret. Dahlia and I will get answers to how this happened."

My heart was racing as I watched the vampire incline his blond head to Kaitlyn before he faced the shadowed court-yard Lucas pointed out earlier and whistled. Several men and women emerged from the shadows and started moving through the mundies still frozen by my spell.

"How are we supposed to find out how this barghest got

here?" I asked Kaitlyn, deciding to focus on the problem I could try and do something about.

Kaitlyn pursed her lips. "We need to talk to Fae and elves that live in the area. I can't imagine any of them traveling to Cottlehill in England and asking for permission to retrieve a barghest. The portal guardians wouldn't allow it even if they had."

My head was pounding, and I was afraid the mixture of smells would trigger my smell-o-vision and make me see something. It was a miracle I hadn't had a premonition yet.

I ran a hand down my face. "Send me a list of Fae and Lucas, and I will go ask some questions."

Kaitlyn clapped a hand on my shoulder. "I'll pay a visit to my friends and see if they heard anything. You go home and rest. Anton and his people have the mundies handled. Everything else can wait."

My shoulder sagged, and I threw my arms around her neck. "Perfect. Thank you."

Kaitlyn nodded and then headed over to Anton. I watched Kaitlyn leave with the vampire right behind her before turning to Lucas. "Why is it that our dates always seem to be interrupted by an angry god or a monster?"

Lucas sighed and brushed my hair away from my face. "I think dark beings are drawn to your light, Flower. It frightens them and makes them want to extinguish it before it burns them to ash."

I snorted as I started walking. "I had no idea I was some kind of lighthouse. I'll have to find a way to dim my beacon, so we can get some peace."

Lucas tugged me into his arms and pressed his lips to mine for a brief yet passionate kiss. "You keep me on my toes. Don't ever try to stifle anything about yourself. I love you no matter what comes our way."

My heart raced as every cell in my body warmed from his

affection. I hadn't dreamed of having a partner like Lucas. My first husband, Leo, wasn't perfect. He tried to make me conform to what he preferred in many ways. Lucas was the first to accept me as I was. And want to keep me that way.

"Good because we need to find out what's going on with the Fae in the French Quarter." Experience told me that the attack by the Fae monster was just the beginning. If Marie was behind the latest, things were about to get ugly, fast.

ABOUT THE AUTHOR

Reviews are like hugs. Sometimes awkward. Always welcome! It would mean the world to me if you can take five minutes and let others know how much you enjoyed my work.

Don't forget to visit my website: www.brendatrim.com and sign up for my newsletter, which is jam-packed with exciting news and monthly giveaways. Also, be sure to visit and like my Facebook page https://www.facebook.com/AuthorBrendaTrim to see my daily posts.

Never allow waiting to become a habit. Live your dreams and take risks. Life is happening now.

DREAM BIG!

XOXO,

Brenda

ALSO BY BRENDA TRIM

The Dark Warrior Alliance

Dream Warrior (Dark Warrior Alliance, Book 1)

Mystik Warrior (Dark Warrior Alliance, Book 2)

Pema's Storm (Dark Warrior Alliance, Book 3)

Isis' Betrayal (Dark Warrior Alliance, Book 4)

Deviant Warrior (Dark Warrior Alliance, Book 5)

Suvi's Revenge (Dark Warrior Alliance, Book 6)

Mistletoe & Mayhem (Dark Warrior Alliance, Novella)

Scarred Warrior (Dark Warrior Alliance, Book 7)

Heat in the Bayou (Dark Warrior Alliance, Novella, Book 7.5)

Hellbound Warrior (Dark Warrior Alliance, Book 8)

Isobel (Dark Warrior Alliance, Book 9)

Rogue Warrior (Dark Warrior Alliance, Book 10)

Shattered Warrior (Dark Warrior Alliance, Book 11)

King of Khoth (Dark Warrior Alliance, Book 12)

Ice Warrior (Dark Warrior Alliance, Book 13)

Fire Warrior (Dark Warrior Alliance, Book 14)

Ramiel (Dark Warrior Alliance, Book 15)

Rivaled Warrior (Dark Warrior Alliance, Book 16)

Dragon Knight of Khoth (Dark Warrior Alliance, Book 17)

Ayil (Dark Warrior Alliance, Book 18)

Guild Master (Dark Alliance Book 19)

Maven Warrior (Dark Alliance Book 20)

Sentinel of Khoth (Dark Alliance Book 21)

Araton (Dark Warrior Alliance Book 22)

Cambion Lord (Dark Warrior Alliance Book 23)

Omega (Dark Warrior Alliance Book 24)

Dark Warrior Alliance Boxsets:

Dark Warrior Alliance Boxset Books 1-4

Dark Warrior Alliance Boxset Books 5-8

Dark Warrior Alliance Boxset Books 9-12

Dark Warrior Alliance Boxset Books 13-16

Dark Warrior Alliance Boxset Books 17-20

Hollow Rock Shifters:

Captivity, Hollow Rock Shifters Book 1

Safe Haven, Hollow Rock Shifters Book 2

Alpha, Hollow Rock Shifters Book 3

Ravin, Hollow Rock Shifters Book 4

Impeached, Hollow Rock Shifters Book 5

Anarchy, Hollow Rock Shifters Book 6

Midlife Witchery:

Magical New Beginnings

Mind Over Magical Matters

Magical Twist

My Magical Life to Live

Forged in Magical Fire

Like a Fine Magical Wine

Magical Yule Tidings

Mystical Midlife in Maine

Magical Makeover

Laugh Lines & Lost Things

Hellmouths & Hot Flashes

Holidays with Hades

Bramble's Edge Academy:

Unearthing the Fae King

Masking the Fae King

Revealing the Fae King

Midnight Doms:

Her Vampire Bad Boy

Her Vampire Suspect

All Souls Night

Printed in Great Britain
by Amazon